He was nak

Her breath escaped ... naked. From the to ... ... tanned feet and everything ... -in between. And—she gulped—there certainly was a *lot* of in between.

She must have made a sound, because Chase stopped shaking water from his hair and lifted his head, his stormy eyes zeroing in on her with laser-point accuracy.

Eve's gaze flew upward and her mind came to a screeching halt.

For a long, breathless moment they stared at each other, the memory of last night like a blaze across the fifteen feet separating them. Finally an arrogant dark brow rose up his bruised forehead, galvanizing Eve into action. She squeaked out an *'Oh!'* slapped a hand over her eyes in delayed reaction and half spun away, aware that her entire body had gone hot. Because the image had been burned onto her brain for all time.

An amused baritone drawled, 'Enjoying the view?' and Eve could have kicked herself for reacting like a ninth-grader caught in the boys' locker room.

'What…what the heck are you d-doing?' she squeaked.

There was a rustle of fabric, then his amused voice drawled, 'It's safe now, Dr Prim. You can look.'

Eve's eyes snapped open and she found him barely a foot away, looking all cool and damp and…*amused*, darn him. But 'safe' was hardly a word she'd use in co... ... a ... aura su... ... ooking as ...

Dear Reader,

With life so hectic, I often wish I could transport myself to a South Seas island for a personal time-out and regain my sanity. Instead I decided to send my very stressed and focussed heroine there to find herself. And it wouldn't be any kind of adventure without a little danger, because we all know that a good crisis shows us what we're made of.

Fortunately Eve is made of stern stuff—she's had plenty of opportunity to toughen up—and she sails through a violent storm and a crash landing with minor scrapes and bruises. But what she finds in the middle of the South Pacific challenges her closely guarded heart in every possible way.

I had such fun writing Eve and Chase's story that I feel I had my time-out in paradise. I hope you do too.

Happy reading,

Lucy

CAUGHT IN A STORM OF PASSION

BY
LUCY RYDER

Published in Great Britain 2016
By Mills & Boon, an imprint of HarperCollins*Publishers*
1 London Bridge Street, London, SE1 9GF

ISBN: 978-0-263-25443-3

Our policy is to use papers that are natural, renewable and recyclable products and made from wood grown in sustainable forests. The logging and manufacturing processes conform to the legal environmental regulations of the country of origin.

Printed and bound in Spain
by CPI, Barcelona

With two beautiful daughters, **Lucy Ryder** had to curb her adventurous spirit and settle down. But because she's easily bored by routine she turned to writing as a creative outlet, and to romances because 'What else is there other than chocolate?' Characterised by friends and family as a romantic cynic, Lucy can't write serious stuff to save her life. She loves creating characters who are funny, romantic and just a little cynical.

Books by Lucy Ryder

Mills & Boon Medical Romance

Resisting Her Rebel Hero
Tamed by Her Army Doc's Touch
Falling at the Surgeon's Feet

Visit the Author Profile page at
millsandboon.co.uk for more titles.

This book is dedicated to my niece and nephew,
Cassandra and Sean Bassett, who are about to make
me a great-aunt. I can't wait to meet the new addition
to our awesomely crazy family.
What a lucky kid to have you two as parents.

And also to my sister Jennifer Hargreaves, who needs
a BIG hug and a lot of love and romance of her own.
I love you, Jen.

Praise for
Lucy Ryder

CHAPTER ONE

Tuamotu Archipelago—South Pacific

DR. EVELYN CARMICHAEL squeezed her eyes shut, dug her fingernails into the armrests either side of her and thanked God for the harness strapped across her chest. The large seaplane slewed sideways in the storm that had appeared out of nowhere, just an hour out of Port Laurent. All she could think was, *I'm going to die... I'm going to die in the middle of the South Pacific and I've never had a halfway decent...well...that.*

A monster gust of wind hit the aircraft broadside, threatening to shake everything loose. Metal screamed under the assault, as though the agony of it was too much to bear in stoic silence. Eve could empathize. She was all too ready to start screaming herself. And she would if she had the presence of mind to do anything but sit wide-eyed with terror as the world around her went to hell.

A good thing too, since being frozen with terror kept her from freaking out. Because, frankly, she'd rather die than give the man beside her—the pilot from hell—the pleasure of seeing her fall apart.

She didn't look out the cockpit window and she didn't look sideways at the heathen turning the air blue. He was big and scary enough, without the palpable tension pouring off him between curses.

And, boy, were his curses inventive. Some she'd never heard before…others she never would have *thought*, let alone uttered. But they rolled off his tongue like they were best buddies.

Fortunately he seemed to have forgotten her in his battle with the aircraft and Mother Nature. Which suited her just fine. It meant he was too busy to witness her mental meltdown.

Again.

A few hours earlier she'd opened her eyes and realized she was lying on a rattan sofa with a big half-naked sea god looming over her. Wide shouldered and long legged, he'd filled the space with a toxic cocktail of masculine superiority and supreme sexual confidence. She'd hated him instantly.

Of course it had absolutely nothing to do with the unwelcome shiver of almost primal awareness his proximity had sent zinging through her veins, but rather the abrupt knowledge that he'd seen her at her most helpless.

And if there was one thing Eve hated it was being helpless.

Fine. It might also have had something to do with the way he'd made her feel—like she was awkward and gawky and thirteen again. Like she had to pretend she wasn't dressed in charity-shop rejects and the object of pity or derision.

She'd only had to look at him, leaning close and dripping water all over her, to know he'd put the *bad* in bad boy.

Fortunately for Eve she was no longer shy or geeky, and she'd never had a thing for bad boys. That had been her mother's weakness and one she'd vowed never to share. Besides, she was a thirty-year-old recently qualified OB-GYN specialist, on the brink of a promising career, and she'd learned early on that a cool look and a raised brow quickly dispelled any unwelcome ideas.

But this…this Neanderthal, with his hard body, cool

gray eyes and his soft cargoes worn in interesting places, had found her icy looks amusing. His eyebrow had arched with more mockery than she could ever hope to muster.

He'd promptly sent her blood pressure soaring into the stratosphere—and not just with aggravation. That, as far as Eve was concerned, was reason enough to hate him.

But none of that *really* mattered. Not when her entire life was flashing before her eyes—which were still squeezed tightly closed, to shut out the vision of her impending death.

"Just stay calm!" her pilot shouted above the roar of the storm and the screech of tortured metal.

"I *am* calm," she snarled, snapping her eyes open to glare at him. And she could have promptly kicked herself when he turned those disturbing slate-gray eyes her way and she got a little light-headed.

From jet lag, worry and exhaustion, she assured herself. Or maybe it was from all the testosterone that surrounded him like a thick toxic cloud. She was clearly allergic. All she needed was the antihistamine, hidden somewhere in her luggage, and she'd be fine.

Hopefully immune.

Oh, wait. Her suitcase was MIA. Along with her mind for even starting on this wild goose chase in the first place.

"Is that why you're whimpering?"

His mouth twitched and she was tempted to snarl at him again, maybe use her teeth. She'd never been a violent person, but she would make an exception with him. Unfortunately he was about as sensitive as a rock, and any biting on her part would in all probability be construed as interest.

"Just keep this flying boat in the air, Slick, and let me handle my own life flashes."

"We're going to be okay, I promise," he said. "Chris has never failed me, and I've flown in *much* worse."

She didn't know how that could be possible, but who the heck was she to judge? She could take or leave flying on a good day, and this certainly wasn't turning out to be one of them. Besides, after a lifetime of disappointments she never put much store in empty promises, and his promise to keep them safe was as about as empty as the sky had been a half-hour earlier.

"You named your seaplane Chris? So what's it short for? Christine? Crystal?" She smirked. "Christian?"

He sent her a *get real* look that questioned her intelligence before flicking the Saint Christopher medal hanging overhead with one long tanned finger.

"Saint Chris. We have an understanding."

She wished he had an understanding with the weather, instead of a piece of metal that had about as much magic as this flying boat.

The thought had only just formed when the world exploded in a blinding flash of blue-white light. She sucked in a terrified squeak and nearly scorched her lungs on white-hot sulfur an instant before sparks shot out of the control panel. They were almost instantly followed by ominous pop-popping sounds.

"Oh, great!"

"What?" Back ramrod straight, she turned huge eyes on her pilot. His face was grimmer than the Grim Reaper and the death grip he had on the joystick didn't fill her with a lot of confidence. *"What?"*

"Dammit, don't just sit there," he snapped, his hands flying over the instruments. "Grab the fire extinguisher."

"We're on fire?" Eve felt her mouth drop open. She stared at him in horror. *They were fifteen hundred feet above the sea, for God's sake.* They couldn't be on fire. She was *not* going to fry in a flying fireball.

"Flames are coming out the damn control panel, woman," he barked. "Of course we're on fire. *Now, get the extinguisher."*

"I thought you said we were going to be okay. You *promised*!" Eve could hear herself, but she was unable to move or keep the abject horror and panic from her voice.

She—who never panicked—was about to lose it.

"Dear God, we're going to die. I knew this was a bad idea. But did I listen?"

"We are *not* going to die. And I always keep my promises."

He caught her horrified gaze with his, and the burning intensity of his eyes was strangely hypnotizing.

"Always," he growled fervently. "Now, snap out of it and get the damn extinguisher."

In a daze, Eve fumbled for the buckle and wondered if it was such a good idea to leave her seat. Maybe the fire would go out on its own. Maybe he could smother it with his damn ego. Besides, her hands were shaking so badly it was several seconds before the mechanism gave and her safety harness snapped open.

She hadn't signed up for this, she told herself, struggling to hang on to her composure. It was all just a bad dream. She was supposed to be in London, sitting in a posh hotel, attending the Women and Birth conference. Actually she *had* been in London—for all of two hours—before catching the first flight out of Heathrow because her sister had left a message saying she'd met someone and was getting married.

Married! To a guy she'd only just met. In the South Pacific, for crying out loud. Had Amelia lost her mind? Had she learned nothing from their dysfunctional childhood?

There would be no marriage, Eve vowed fervently. At least not yet. Because if her sister *had* lost her mind, as the older twin it was up to Eve to help her find it again. Besides, Eve had a lifetime's experience of watching over her sweet, trusting sibling and she wasn't going to stop now. Especially with the kind of men Amelia seemed to attract. Men quick to take advantage of her naive and generous soul. Like the men parading through their mother's life.

Clearly being on a tropical island was messing with Amelia's mind just as it had their mother's, when she'd met and fallen head over heels in lust with their father. Just another man in a long line of users and abusers. All Eve had to do was fly out there, talk some sense into her twin and fly back to London in time for the last three days of the conference...preferably with her sister in tow. It would be just like their childhood. Just the two of them against the world.

Only now she might not make it to the conference. *Or* to Tukamumu to stop the wedding. Or was it Moratunga?

Oh, what the heck difference did it make, anyway? She wasn't going to make either of them because she was headed for a watery grave.

Feeling drunk in the violently pitching craft, she lurched upright and staggered to the fire extinguisher mounted behind the pilot's seat. Not an easy task in three-inch heels.

"Dammit, woman. Move!"

The words were delivered through clenched teeth, and Eve would have liked to tell him to stuff it. But what if he took her at her word and bailed out with the only working parachute? She didn't even want to consider what would happen then.

She yanked at the cylinder, shrieking as the plane took a nosedive. Lurching backward, she hit the cockpit wall and sent foam spraying everywhere.

Everywhere but the fire.

"What the seven levels of hell are you doing?" he bellowed, reaching back to grab a fistful of her silk blouse and yanking her upright.

She would have liked to tell him that he was manhandling two hundred dollars' worth of silk, but staying on her feet was more of a priority.

"The *fire*," he snarled, looking more scary than comical with foam in his hair and dripping off his nose and chin. "Aim the nozzle at the damn fire."

"Maybe you should keep the damn floor from moving," Eve snapped with extreme provocation, and slapped at the hand dangerously close to her breasts. Only it turned out to be a mistake when the floor abruptly tilted again and she tumbled into his lap—a tangle of arms, legs, nozzle and extinguisher.

Eve shrieked and attempted not to conk him on the head with the canister, because an unconscious pilot was something she wanted to avoid. At all costs. She whacked herself instead, instantly seeing stars and wondering if her life really was flashing before her eyes.

Dammit. It figured that she'd die in the arms of a man more interested in shoving her away than wrapping her close.

Yelping, she let the extinguisher go to slap a hand over the injury and thought, *Great—another bruise to go with the one I already have thanks to Mr. I'm-your-pilot, Chase.* There was a soft grunt, followed by a vicious oath, and the next thing she was being dumped on her ass. Through tearing eyes she saw him aim the nozzle at the controls with one hand while yanking at the yoke with the other. Within seconds the instruments were covered with a thick layer of foam.

The fire gave one last defiant fizzle before dying.

Kind of like her last relationship, she thought dazedly from her position on the floor. Actually, kind of like *all* her relationships, if she was being perfectly honest, because watching her mother flit from one man to the next had soured her when it came to love. She snorted. As if whatever her mother had had with her countless men had been *love*.

Relief, however, was short-lived, because no sooner had Chase tossed the canister aside than he wrapped both white-knuckled hands around the yoke, looked at the instruments now oozing white foam and cursed.

Again.

Eve didn't like the look on his face.

"Now what?"

His expression was taut and grim, his eyes narrowed in

fierce concentration. A muscle twitched in his lean, tanned cheek.

"Don't you dare tell me we're going down," she informed him tightly. "Because you'll have a hysterical female on your hands. And you do *not* want to see me hysterical."

He shot her a look that said she'd sailed past hysterical a half hour ago. She ignored him. They were going down. *She* knew it. *He* knew it. He was just too darn stubborn and macho to admit that Saint Chris had abandoned them.

She swallowed a sob.

And here she was in the prime of her life, on the verge of a promising career—the realization of all her dreams after years of hard work.

She had every right to be hysterical, darn it.

Grabbing the seat, she hauled herself up. He was back to ignoring her, wrestling with the controls and trying to bring the plane's nose up through sheer brute force.

And failing.

Oh, God, he was failing, and the nose was pointing down into what she knew would be a very unpleasant end. They might be in a seaplane, and not at the altitude of a commercial jet, but that would mean nothing when they hit the water at a sixty-degree angle. Besides, she'd watched all those seconds-from-disaster documentaries and knew there'd be no floating gently away from this.

Gulping, Eve watched in terrified fascination as the muscles in his arms and shoulders bunched and strained against his soft polo shirt and smooth, tanned flesh until she thought they'd burst right out of his skin.

"Buckle up," he snarled through clenched teeth. "It's going to get rough."

Eve felt her mouth drop open. More than it was already? A whimper bubbled up her throat and threatened to pop, along with her very tenuous hold on control. She was absolutely certain she could not handle rough.

They were going down.

"We're going to die."

"We are *not* going to die. I'm an excellent pilot," he said tightly, and the engines protested with an almost human scream.

"In case you haven't noticed, *Slick*," Eve yelped, almost as loudly as the engines as she fought with the safety harness that seemed to have taken on an evil life of its own, "this is not a storm for excellent pilots. It isn't even for creatures *meant* to fly. It's Armageddon. And if I die I'm going to kill you. Very. Very. Slowly."

"I have no intention of dying," he snapped, as though she'd insulted his manhood as well as his entire family tree. "And what kind of doctor are *you* to be threatening the man trying to save your delectable ass, anyway?"

He shook his head at her and reached out to snag his Saint Christopher, kissing it before he looped it around his neck.

Eve watched in fascination as the shiny silver disc disappeared into the neckline of his shirt, wondering at her brief flash of envy that Saint Chris got to be nestled close to his heat and strength.

Dammit. *She* wanted to be held and protected too.

Just this once.

"What *you* need is a little faith," he declared, just as the craft bucked and the engines gave an alarming splutter.

She swallowed another yelp, envy forgotten as she sank her nails into the armrests, wishing it was his hard thigh. She would like to put a few holes in his thick hide, despite the "delectable" quip. Besides, her "delectable ass," as he'd so gallantly put it, was in real danger of becoming shark bait.

"What I *need*," she snarled, "is for you to get us out of this storm. What I need is to find my sister and stop her from making the biggest mistake of her life." Her voice rose. "What I need is not to be thinking about meeting my maker without ever having had a screaming orgas— Well, never mind."

"What?" His gaze whipped to hers so fast she half expected his head to fly off his shoulders. After a moment his gaze dropped to her mouth. "A *what*?"

"Never mind," she squeaked, losing her famed cool just a little. "I am *not* discussing the fact that I'm nearly thirty-one years old and have never had an earth-shaking orgasm. Before I kick the bucket I'd like to have just one. *One!*" Her voice rose. "Is that too much to ask?"

"You… *What?*" He looked so stunned that if she hadn't been on the verge of a total meltdown she might have been flattered by his stunned disbelief. Or maybe insulted, since the disbelief was now edged with amusement. It didn't matter that at any other time she would have been mortified at having admitted anything so private. Especially to this heathen flyboy. But since she was going to die she guessed it didn't really matter. Dignity was the least of her problems.

"No. And now I'm *never* going to."

His answer was drowned out by another ear-splitting explosion and in the next instant the airplane lurched sideways and flipped, throwing her violently against the harness. Lights exploded inside her skull and she knew that this was it. She was going to die and she was never going to have that screaming orgasm.

And to think she could be safely in London, with a hundred eligible men…

CHAPTER TWO

Six hours earlier, Port Laurent, Tangaroa.

EVELYN PRACTICALLY FELL out of the cab as it came to a screeching halt in front of a squat building professing to be the offices of Tiki Sea & Air Charter Services. She'd flown halfway around the world, but the worst part of the journey by far had been the past five miles. Five miles of absolute white-knuckled terror in a cab that she was somewhat surprised to have survived.

Swaying in the intense midday heat, Eve clutched the side of the car and locked her wobbly knees against the urge to sink to the ground. The only thing stopping her was the knowledge that the road was hotter than the depths of hell and would fry anything on contact. If she didn't get somewhere air-conditioned soon the soles of her elegant heels weren't the only things in danger of vaporizing with a whimper.

She'd left Boston in freezing rain, landed at Heathrow in the middle of a snowstorm, and the smart little suit she'd bought to celebrate her new professional status was sticking to her skin as if she was a sealed gourmet snack. And, since her suitcase had been lost in transit, there was nothing in her overnight bag suitable for the current soaring temperatures and smothering humidity.

Fine. There was nothing in her suitcase either, but at

least she'd have something fresh to change into. She'd lost count of the time zones she'd crossed to get to… *Darn, where the heck was she?*

Blinking, she looked around, but that didn't help because she was in a daze of fatigue and jet lag and couldn't remember the name of the South Pacific island she'd just landed on.

Oh, boy… The South Pacific.

Her pulse picked up, her ears buzzed and a prickly heat erupted over her body. For an awful moment she thought she was going to pass out, and quickly sucked in the warm, moist air to clear her head.

Who'd have thought when she'd stepped off the plane at Heathrow and turned on her phone that instead of heading for the Women and Birth conference, as she'd been supposed to, she'd be getting back on a plane to fly off to Tuka-Tuka.

Or was it Moramumu?

She sighed.

She'd never even *heard* of the Society Islands, let alone a chain called the Tuamotu Archipelago. Which begged the question: what the heck was her sister doing down here? The last she'd heard Amelia had been singing at some fancy hotel in Hawaii.

"Lady, you sure you wanna be here?" the cab driver yelled over the music pumping from the boom box mounted on the dashboard. "There's a much better place on the other side of the marina."

"That's very kind of you," Eve said, hopefully masking her horror at the thought of getting back into that death trap for one mile more than was absolutely necessary. The guy flashed his gold teeth and cackled uproariously, making her think that maybe she hadn't been all that successful in hiding her dismay. But then she was about twenty-nine hours past exhausted and couldn't be expected to control anything more than the urge to weep. Or maybe scream.

And that was only because she was clenching her teeth hard enough to pulverize bone and enamel.

With a cheerfulness that Eve wished *she* felt—she was in the South Pacific, for heaven's sake—the driver wrestled her bag from the cab and dropped it at her feet, along with her heavy winter coat. Then he hopped back into his decrepit vehicle and took off like a lost soul out of hell, singing at the top of his lungs to the song blaring from his boom box.

Sucking in air so heavy with moisture she thought she might be forced to grow gills, Eve hoisted her bag and coat onto her shoulder. Clutching her laptop close, she headed across the road to the small building squatting like a smug hen in a bed of exotic flowers and dense vegetation.

Suddenly she had absolutely no idea what she was doing.

The wooden doors to Tiki Sea & Air were open, and Eve climbed the stone stairs to a wide wraparound porch decorated with hanging baskets exploding with exotic-looking flowers. The heady fragrance reminded her of the perfume counters at Bloomingdale's. Rich, lush and exotic.

Inhaling the humid air, Eve looked around and decided she must be dreaming—heck, she was exhausted enough. It was as if she'd stepped into a brochure advertising glamorous holiday destinations. But since she'd never taken a holiday, let alone been tempted to research one, she couldn't tell for certain.

Okay, that was a lie. She and her sister had used to dream all the time when they were kids about finding some exotic island where they'd live with their father and eat coconuts and fruit and maybe learn to catch fish. A place where they'd be safe and adored.

She snorted. *Yeah, right*. That had been so long ago it might have been someone else's dream. Before she'd stopped believing in fairy tales. Before she'd learned that if she wanted "safe and secure" she'd have to create it herself.

Swiping at a trickle of perspiration, she glanced over to

where an old man lay dozing on an old rattan sofa and experienced a moment of pure envy. She'd be willing to har-
vest her own kidney for a soft bed, clean sheets and about
twenty-four hours of oblivion.

Oh, yeah…and air-conditioning.

She groaned as sweat ran down her throat and disappeared between her breasts. Definitely air-conditioning.

Deciding that she didn't have the energy to fight the
old guy for sofa space, Eve headed for the open door and
stepped into an old French Colonial–style building that
looked about three decades past its sell-by date.

The room looked like something out of a movie. There
was a scattering of worn rattan furnishings, coconut fiber
mats dotting the floor and a large overhead fan that lazily
circulated the heavy air.

A large curved bamboo counter took up most of the far
end of the room, and behind that, through the open slatted
wooden French doors, Eve could see a back porch leading
down to a long, wide wooden dock. Bobbing on the in-
sanely bright turquoise water was a large white seaplane.
Beyond that she could see a headland and the open sea,
sparkling like a trillion jewels in the sun.

Approaching the counter, Eve peered over the scarred
surface, hoping to find someone who could help her. Other
than an empty mug, an overflowing wastebasket and about
a ton of boxes, the only sign of life was a quietly humming
computer and the soft *clunk, clunk, clunk* of the overhead
fan.

She glanced through another open doorway behind the
counter into a small messy office, but it too was deserted.

"Dammit," Eve muttered, huffing out an irritated breath.
"Where the heck *is* everyone?"

A loud, hoarse, *"Ia ora na e Maeva!"* had her jump-
ing about a foot in the air. She looked around, wide-eyed,
for the owner of that raspy voice. But other than the loud

snoring coming from the old man on the front porch the building was quiet.

Quiet and deserted.

Wonderful. Now she was hearing voices on top of everything else.

Telling herself she wasn't losing her grip on reality, Eve dropped her belongings onto a nearby chair and headed for the open doors, determined to find the source of that raspy voice. And hopefully someone who could tell her where to find a pilot named Chase.

She stepped onto the back porch and was instantly blinded by the midday light. Heat rose from the dock and the large bay reflected sunlight like a laser show.

Resisting the urge to retreat inside the blessedly dim building, she lifted a hand to shade her eyes as the raspy voice yelled, *"Ia ora na e Maeva!"* in her ear.

Heart lurching with fright, she swung around, expecting a hatchet-wielding psycho, and found herself face-to-beak with a large bright blue-and-scarlet parrot perched on a tree stump, watching her with baleful eyes.

"Oh!" she said to the bird on an explosive exhalation of relief, and took a cautionary step out of range of the wicked-looking beak. "Hi. Do you know where I can find, um…Chase?"

The bird cocked its head and Eve sighed. Now she was talking to a bird. Which probably meant lack of sleep along with stress and panic was sending her right over the edge.

"Okay. How about your owner?"

The parrot ruffled its bright feathers.

"Anyone?"

"Squaaawk!"

"Fine," she said a little shortly. "I'll just go find him myself, then, shall I?"

"Ma-oo roo-roo ro-aa," the parrot crooned, and bobbed up and down.

"Yeah, you too," she muttered, heading for the porch

railing. She leaned over, looking past the abundant vegetation to follow where wide wooden planks led straight toward a fancy marina and the bustling business center. To her right it disappeared into the cluster of houses perched along the water's edge a couple hundred yards away.

Not a living thing stirred, everything having most likely locked itself away from the suffocating heat.

Feeling a little queasy, Eve sank onto the top step, expelling a weary breath just as a long, tanned arm appeared out of the water and slapped onto the dock.

Almost instantly another appeared, holding a string bag of fish. And then, with both large hands planted on the dock, the rest of him followed—all six foot plus of him—emerging from the bay like a sea god visiting lesser land mortals.

Eve's eyes widened and her mouth dropped open. Her eyes were locked on the gush of water lovingly tracing all that tanned masculine magnificence as it rushed south. *Waaaay* south.

She licked her parched lips, following the streams of water that cascaded over his wide chest and the almost perfect lines of his shoulders and biceps as though lovingly caressing the hard planes it traversed. Moving down spectacular pecs, racing over delineated abs toward the happy trail that disappeared into the waistband of his low-riding board shorts.

Eve sucked in a stunned breath—*holy molasses*—his legs were just as long and tanned and perfect as the rest of him. She blinked as the image wavered and wondered if she was hallucinating. But when he remained, bathed in sunlight that cast his ripped physique in bold relief, she sighed. One of those stupid girlie sighs that would have appalled her if she hadn't been on the very edge of exhaustion.

Wow… just *wow!*

Unaware of her fascinated gaze, the sea god shook his head like a dog, water flying off in all directions, before stooping to retrieve the string bag in one effortless move. He turned and headed up the dock toward her, his free hand wiping water from his face.

Eve knew the instant he saw her. His body stilled for just a heartbeat, and if her gaze hadn't been locked on him like a laser she would have missed that barely perceptible pause. Without breaking stride, he resumed that loose-hipped lope up the dock, his expression dark and hooded.

Feeling suddenly nervous, Eve rose to her feet and smoothed her hands down her skirt—whether to smooth out the wrinkles or to dry her damp palms, she wasn't sure. Almost instantly there was a loud buzzing in her head. Her vision swam alarmingly, and as if from down a long, hollow tunnel she heard herself say, "I'm Evelyn Carmichael and I'm looking…for…I'm looking for… Ch—"

If there was one thing Chase Gallagher hated more than the IRS, it was big-city career women with big-city attitudes. But even *he* had to admit that the sight of long shapely legs ending in a pair of elegant heels was sexy as hell, and something that he hadn't realized he'd missed.

And because he'd missed it he scowled down at the woman responsible for that unwelcome flash of yearning. He didn't miss the city, or the hectic hours and traffic, and he certainly didn't miss the big-city career attitude. Especially not the kind that made people put career before family. *Hell.* Career before *anything.* Except, of course, when something bigger and better came along.

He'd done that once and it had cost him more than a huge chunk of change.

So even though the sight of his visitor, all her prim tidiness beginning to fray at the edges, had sent his pulse ratcheting up a couple notches, he'd studied her coolly, determined to get rid of her as soon as possible. But that had been before she'd decided to sway on her feet and take a header into the ground, forcing him to leap forward and catch her before she fell.

Medium height, nice curvy body and scraped-back tawny hair that would probably glitter a hundred different colors in the sunlight—if she ever relaxed enough to let her hair down, he thought with a snort. Then a close-up of her face had him sucking in a shocked breath, because for one instant there he'd thought he was staring at his future sister-in-law.

But that was ridiculous, because not only had he left Amelia behind at the resort, with his brother, Jude, *this* woman had big-city impatience stamped all over her and none of Amelia's sunny sweetness.

This had to be Amelia's sister. The evil twin, he told himself as he slid one arm beneath her shoulders and the other beneath her knees.

Lifting her into his arms, Chase ascended the stairs, cursing his bad luck. He'd taken one look at the woman and recognized trouble.

And these days Chase Gallagher avoided trouble.

At least of the feminine variety.

He shook his head at the prim skirt, long-sleeved button-up shirt and nylon-clad legs. *Oh, yeah*—heat exhaustion just waiting to happen. If not for those things, this woman was a dead ringer for his brother's fiancée.

With the parrot leading the way in a flurry of feathers, Chase carried her into the waiting room and laid her down on the rattan sofa that had seen better days. He adjusted a cushion beneath her head and stood back.

He knew he had to do something. What, he didn't know. He knew only that the long-sleeved blouse was still buttoned at her wrists, and in this heat that was a sure-fire way to get heatstroke.

After a brief internal battle Chase cursed and reached out to slip the small buttons free, jolting as the parrot landed on his shoulder, crooning, *"Ia ora na e Maeva,"* in Chase's ear.

"Yeah, welcome to you too, buddy," he said in relief.

Ignoring the flashes of lace and silk was easier with the bird's talons digging into his shoulder, reminding him that tugging the damp shirt and camisole from her waistband was for medical purposes. And not for whatever his mind was suddenly conjuring up.

He shook his head as much at the woman as at himself. No wonder she'd passed out. She was dressed like a school librarian heading for Congress. And then he couldn't resist a little smile tugging reluctantly at his mouth.

Okay, maybe not a librarian, he thought, hurrying off to find water and a cloth. More like a sexy lawyer hoping to disguise herself as a librarian. He shook his head. No disguising all that creamy skin, or the curves beneath those prim clothes.

He sighed. The nylons would have to go. As would the blouse, or the under-thingy. But first he had to revive her and get some fluids down her throat.

She was moaning softly when he returned with a huge wad of paper toweling and an opened bottle of water. Tearing off a section of paper towel, he soaked it with cool water before wiping her clammy forehead.

The pulse at the base of her throat fluttered wildly; her breathing was rapid and shallow.

Great. Just great. Maybe he should just take her to the hospital and let them deal with her. Maybe he should just fly outta here and tell Amelia her sister hadn't shown.

Yeah, and maybe he wouldn't do *any* of those things, he thought as he envisioned the scene that would follow. He shuddered. Besides, the last thing he wanted was to see Amelia's big blue eyes shimmering with hurt and know he was the cause.

Soaking another handful of towels, he roughly bathed the woman's clammy skin, careful not to let his eyes wander to those tempting mounds of creamy flesh barely contained in silk and lace. If she suddenly woke up he didn't want to be caught eyeing the goodies.

First, she wasn't his type—*so not your type, Chase*—and second his mother had made sure her sons knew how to treat women with respect. Or else.

His mouth twisted as an unpleasant memory arose. Pity his ex-wife hadn't had the same upbringing. Maybe then she wouldn't have had a long-term affair with her boss and blamed Chase's job and his family for the alienation of her affection.

He snorted. *Yeah, right.* As if making mounds of cash trading stocks and bonds was remotely alienating. *He* was the one who should have sued the damn lawyer, but by the time he'd recovered from the shock of betrayal he'd realized he didn't care enough.

He'd survived the unpleasant discovery that his wife loved his money more than she'd loved him. But discovering that Avery had knowingly tried to pass off the Mercer Island shark's baby as his had been like a gut punch.

Fortunately he wasn't as stupid as he looked, and when he'd demanded a paternity test the whole ugly truth had come spewing out. What had really sickened him was the fact that whenever he'd previously brought up the subject of starting a family she'd always claimed that she wasn't ready, that a baby would ruin her career and her figure.

After that he'd left Seattle and moved out here to the islands. He still ran his brokering business, from what his brother called his "bunker"—a windowless, climate-controlled room that housed his huge bank of computers. It was from there that he kept in contact with the financial world and the rest of his Seattle-based family.

But his marriage was in the past and really not worth dwelling on. If he did, he might just dump Amelia's sister in the ocean, head off to his island retreat and pretend none of this had happened. But he really liked his almost sister-in-law, and he was fairly certain Jude wouldn't be happy if he ditched her twin.

In the meantime, what the hell was he supposed to do with an unconscious woman heading for heat exhaustion? Other than strip her and toss her in the bay, that is.

Shoving a hand through his hair, he was contemplating his options when she moaned again. His gaze whipped upward in time to see the long, lush fringe of her dark eyelashes flutter and then lift, exposing glassy eyes the exact color of the five-hundred-dollar bottle of single malt whiskey he kept for special occasions.

Holy—

Air whooshed from his lungs as if he'd been punched in the head. He'd only ever seen eyes like that once before. Twice, actually. Once on an ancient amber Viking ring he'd seen in a museum and the second time…his friend's eyes. But looking into Dr. Alain Broussard's eyes didn't normally leave him reeling like a drunken penguin.

Maybe *he* was the one in need of medical assistance.

She blinked and murmured a husky, "Hi," her expression so softly sensuous that for an instant Chase was startled. Okay, stunned. Because…*jeez*…that look had reached out and grabbed him in a place that hadn't been grabbed since his ex. Maybe even before.

In the next instant the sleepy expression cleared and any resemblance either to Amelia or Alain vanished. Soft and sensuous was replaced by razor-sharp intellect. And outrage.

"What…what the hell are you *doing*?" she demanded, the formerly husky voice full of indignation as she slapped at his hands, which had paused in the task of sponging her down.

Water dripped off the wad and soaked the silk camisole right over her left breast, drawing his fascinated gaze. She must have followed his eyes because she squeaked, shoved at his hand and lurched upright. Unfortunately he didn't

move back fast enough, and her head smacked into his
cheekbone with enough force to rattle his brain.

She gave an agonized yelp, slapped a hand to her head
and sank back against the cushions, moaning as if he'd gut-
ted her with a dull spoon.

Oh, wait—the groaning was coming from *him*.

"What the *hell*, lady?" he snarled, holding his cheek as
he staggered backward and abruptly sat on the old rattan
coffee table, which immediately groaned under his weight.

The move also knocked over the bottled water. He made
a grab for it, only to have it sail through the air, spraying
water in a wide arc. Most of it landed on her—soaking her
already wet camisole. And…*oh, man*…rendering the thin
silk almost transparent. Which he might have appreciated
if she hadn't just tried to head butt him to death.

She made a kind of squeaking, gasping sound and he
saw wide amber eyes glaring at him through a haze of pain.
Realizing he was still holding a wad of damp paper towels,
he slapped it over the lump already forming on his cheek.

"What…what the hell was that for?" he demanded,
checking for blood.

"You…you…" she gasped, and then she turned an interesting shade of green. "Uh-oh." She gulped and slapped
a palm over her mouth. A look of panic crossed her face.
She sat up. "I think I'm… Oh!"

Understanding that garbled sentence, Chase surged to
his feet, scooped her up and rushed down the short passage
to the ladies' bathroom. He shoved the door open with his
shoulder as she made horrifying gagging sounds.

"Hold on a sec—nearly there," he urged in panic, rushing into a stall and dumping her unceremoniously on her
feet. In one smooth move he pushed her head over the toilet, with a firm hand on the back of her neck.

Unresisting, she sank to her knees, her body racked with
a couple dozen dry heaves that made the sweat pop out

across his forehead. He swallowed hard and retreated outside the stall. Just to give her some privacy, he told himself.

After a while there was silence, and when he heard a
weak moan he stuck his head inside. She'd sagged against
the wall, eyes closed as she wiped a limp wrist across her
mouth. Tendrils of hair clung to her damp forehead and
cheeks. She looked so miserable that Chase felt an unwelcome tug of empathy.

Dammit, he thought, shoving a hand through his hair. He
didn't want to feel *anything*—let alone empathy. He'd get
stupid and act like he had rescue issues, for God's sake—
which, come to think of it, was how he'd met Avery.

Yeesh. What an idiot. He'd been a perfect mark. But
he'd learnt a valuable lesson and he wasn't about to repeat his biggest mistake ever. Not now that he was older
and wiser. Not now that he'd learned exactly how devious
women could be.

Eyeing her pasty face with increasing concern, he
crouched beside her. "You okay?"

"I'm…fine…" she rasped, and licked dry lips. "I just
need a—"

"Another moment?" he supplied helpfully when her
words ended abruptly. "A doctor?"

"Don't…don't be ridiculous," she scoffed huskily, plant-
ing one hand on the toilet and the other on his shoulder.

Her touch had him thinking bad thoughts, especially
when his body stirred.

"I *am* a doctor." She tried to push herself to her feet but
she was still weak and shaky and immediately slid back
down.

He eyed her suspiciously as an unpleasant thought occurred to him. Fainting? Vomiting? It was exactly what
had happened to Avery when—

"Are you pregnant?" he demanded abruptly.

Her head whipped up and her mouth dropped open.
"What—? *No!*"

She looked so insulted that he should suggest such a thing that his breath escaped in a loud *whoosh*. He wasn't entirely sure why her reaction relieved him—for all he knew she could be lying. And boy did he have enough experience with *that*!

Slipping his hand beneath her armpit, he rose, drawing her to her feet. She instantly sagged against him, legs wobbly as a newborn calf. Instead of pushing her away he drew her closer, enjoying her soft, warm scent and the feel of her plump breasts against his naked chest.

Realizing what he was doing, he quickly backed out of the stall and led her to the counter, shoving her into a chair while he ripped paper towels from the dispenser. He gave the tap a vicious little twist and thrust the wad into the stream of water that appeared.

What the hell was that? Maybe the heat was affecting him too, because no way could he be attracted to her. Not only was she a big-city woman, she was almost his *sister*, for cripes' sake.

Well, her sister was. Which was the same thing. Wasn't it?

His breath whooshed out. *Hell.*

He turned to find her watching him with those solemn golden-syrup eyes and felt his gut clench with something hot and wild. Something along the lines of golden syrup and…and acres of soft naked skin.

The reaction shook him.

Realizing he was standing there like an idiot, he tore his gaze away, feeling the tips of his ears burn. She was the last person he wanted to feel anything for. Which just went to show that abstinence made people crazy.

Hoping to restore his IQ, he thrust the dripping mess of paper in her direction and eyed her out of the corner of his eyes.

"If you're a doctor, what the hell are you doing in the South Pacific dressed like…*that*?" He waved his arm, sending drops of water flying. "That's an open invitation to de-hydration and heat exhaustion."

She eyed the sodden mass for a couple beats before lift-ing her gaze, her expression rife with annoyance and maybe her opinion of his medical skills.

It wasn't in the least complimentary. So why the hell did Chase feel his lips twitch?

There was nothing amusing about this. Nothing at all. And he certainly wasn't attracted to her. No way. She was too uptight for his liking, and she literally vibrated with exhaustion and impatience.

After a couple more beats she sighed and rose shakily to her feet. Taking the towels from him, she sagged weakly against the counter, where she dumped the sloppy mess and reached for the dispenser.

"Maybe because I was on my way to a conference in London when I got a very disturbing message about my sister getting married to a man she's only just met. A loser who's probably taking advantage of her right this minute. *And*," she added, sending him a look in the mirror that questioned the size of his brain, "in case you think every-one lives in perpetual summer, the northern hemisphere is experiencing a season called *winter*. I left Boston in freez-ing rain and landed in a London blizzard."

"Well, *that*—" he gestured rudely to her once-snazzy outfit, outraged by the nasty quip about his brother "—will have to go, or you'll be fainting on me every five minutes." Jude wasn't the kind of guy to take advantage of women, more like the other way around.

She made a growling sound in the back of her throat and her narrowed gaze snapped up to lock on his in the mirror. Her expression didn't bode well for his continued good health.

He barely managed to cover his grin with another frown. *Dammit.* What the hell was wrong with him?

"I did not faint," she said slowly, precisely. As though he was a few bricks short of a wall.

He snorted, beginning to enjoy himself. "Could have fooled me."

Her eyes narrowed further. "I never faint. Anyway, why do *you* care? It's not like we're ever going to see each other again after I fly out of here."

Her tone suggested she couldn't wait for that moment, so he sighed and pushed away from the counter. Yeah, well, neither could he. But that wasn't about to happen.

For either of them.

His enjoyment abruptly vanished.

"Uh-huh?" he drawled, heading for the door, where he paused, turning to find an odd expression on her face as she watched him leave. "And how do you plan to fly out of here, Your Highness? Grow a pair of wings?"

"Don't be absurd. I'm looking for Chase…something or other." She frowned and lifted pale unsteady fingers to the bruise already forming on her forehead.

He tried not to feel guilty for putting it there as it had mostly been *her* fault. Besides, his eye was also swelling, and his cheek hurt like hell.

Her hand dropped to clutch the counter, as though she was a little dizzy. She sucked in a deep breath that just about gave him a heart attack as those creamy mounds of flesh rose above the lace-trimmed camisole. It was several seconds before he realized that while he was having some very racy thoughts, she was gaping at him with dawning horror.

"*You're* Chase, aren't you?"

For a long moment he stared at her with an odd feeling clenching his gut. It wasn't exactly fear. Because he wasn't afraid of anything. Not Chase Gallagher. Nuh-uh. No way. And certainly not of a city woman.

He snorted. Especially not *this* city woman, with her tawny hair, creamy skin and large whiskey eyes. She was going to be his brother's sister-in-law, for God's sake. Which made her practically family. And if there was one thing a Gallagher didn't do it was leave family—no matter what.

"Don't be too long," he ordered over his shoulder. "Our lunch should be here soon, and I need to load the cargo before we leave."

CHAPTER THREE

The crash site—Moratunga Island, one hundred miles north of Tukamumu.

CHASE BECAME AWARE of two things simultaneously. The wind and the pain. The former was slashing at his face along with needlelike rain, and the latter...*jeez*...was threatening to explode his brains all over the inside of his skull.

He gave a rough groan and fought the urge to empty his stomach. On the bright side, pain meant that he was alive. Which was good, he mused drowsily as he began drifting off into comforting darkness. Real good. Alive meant it had all been a bad dream...

He jerked awake, his heart lurching into a dead run as his gaze flew around the cockpit and he realized something was wrong with this picture. He instantly knew it was the wrong move when pain tore through his head and the smell of burnt plastic made him gag.

Fire!

The thought had him grabbing for his harness, which he released an instant before he realized he was hanging practically upside down.

The controls broke his fall, his left shoulder taking most of the impact before he slid to the floor in a groaning heap.

Holy freaking moly!

Chase lay dazed for a couple minutes, his shoulder radiating pain and fire, his head throbbing like an open wound. Finally his vision cleared enough to recognize that there was—*what the hell?*—vegetation growing inside his best girl.

Either he was hallucinating or—

The storm!

Oh, yeah.

He sucked in a breath when memories rushed back. The crash.

He'd crashed his plane.

Un-be-freaking-lievable.

Muttering curses about stupid storms that weren't supposed to change direction so fast, Chase grabbed his shoulder and sat up. His stomach instantly revolted and he froze. Okay. Note to self. No moving until the nightmare faded.

When it didn't, he sucked in a careful breath and blinked up into the darkness, wondering why there were two mannequins hanging a foot from his face. He knew for a fact there were no mannequins on the cargo manifest.

Then he realized that he was seeing double, and that he was looking at… What the heck was her name? He squinted past the pain and caught sight of a cascade of tawny gold hair a few feet away. His heart surged into his throat as he recognized… Amelia? Dammit, his brother was going to— *No, wait.* Not Amelia. *Evelyn*—Amelia's evil twin— and her arms, legs and hair were hanging limply from the harness.

"Eve…Evelyn?" he rasped, wondering how long he'd been out. A couple of minutes? Hours? Vaguely alarmed by her utter stillness, he cleared his throat and tried again. "Hey, Doc!"

Nothing. Not even the slightest of movements. He sucked in air, shoving down panic, and attempted to squelch the awful thought that came with the dread. His heart pounded. No, no, *no*! No way was the feisty doc—

"Eve! Wake up, *dammit*."

Head spinning, and nausea clawing its way into his throat, Chase hauled himself upright with his good arm. The world tilted, along with his stomach, and he braced himself between the chair and the controls until the urge to vomit settled. Not only did the thought of all that cool fire being extinguished leave a bitter taste of loss in his mouth, it filled him with a sudden hollow desolation he couldn't explain.

They'd only just *met*, for cripes' sake, and he didn't even like her. But she was his responsibility—not to mention his future sister-in-law, sort of—and the first thing he needed to do was check her vitals.

He fumbled beneath that thick curtain of tawny hair and searched for a pulse. When he found it, in the soft spot just beneath her jawline, his breath whooshed out with relief at the strong and steady rhythm.

She was alive.

With the realization dawning on him that they'd just cheated certain death, Chase reached into his shirt with unsteady hands. His fingers encountered the Saint Christopher and he pulled it out, pausing to give it a noisy, grateful kiss.

Thank God she was alive and breathing.

He was breathing too, which meant that when he checked her over for other injuries he got a little sidetracked by the sight of the long naked legs…all four of them…which any red-blooded man would have noticed. Two of the four feet were bare, and her ivory silk blouse had worked loose from her skirt, exposing a few inches of skin that suddenly seemed more erotic than if she was naked.

Which was just plain stupid. He lived in paradise, where women wore a heck of a lot less in public. Besides, he had way more important things to obsess about. Like the fact that she was still unconscious. Like the fact that he'd crashed his damn airplane…well, somewhere.

Hell! He couldn't believe it. He'd flown these waters for almost five years without a single incident.

Shoving unsteady fingers through his hair, Chase looked around and tried to come to terms with reality. It couldn't be a coincidence, he told himself wildly, that the day she'd practically thrown herself into his arms and then tried to head butt him to death, *this* had happened.

The woman was bad luck.

One he needed to avoid. Like a death plague.

Besides, she was uptight and anal—his *least* favorite type of woman. "The type of woman I moved thousands of miles to get away from," he informed the unconscious woman irritably. "The last thing I need complicating my life."

Even temporarily.

So why the hell was he so fascinated by her damn-your-hide attitude and glowing amber eyes?

Biting back a curse at his idiocy, Chase massaged his throbbing temple and ordered himself not to think about underwear. But the more he tried *not* to think about lace and silk, the more he recalled his first glimpse of her heart-shaped butt, encased in that tight soft green skirt, bent over the bathroom counter at Port Laurent.

It had sparked some pretty racy fantasies that had just about fried his brain. And before he'd known it his gaze had been sliding down a pair of spectacular legs more suited to a Vegas showgirl than a workaholic doctor.

He'd blamed it on testosterone and abstinence, of course.

And now possibly concussion—because the sedate little business suit would have looked perfectly respectable on anyone who didn't have enough curves to rival the Indy 500 race track.

Obviously living like a monk made a guy think about sex even when he'd just crashed his plane. Obviously he'd hit his head *really* hard. Maybe he even had brain damage.

Well...hell.

Too bad Mother Nature had decided to have a little fun with him, he thought darkly, swiping at a trickle of something warm and sticky on his face. She'd fried the right engine and most of the electronics. And if that wasn't bad enough she'd made him look bad in front of this sexy, uptight doc after he'd promised her everything was going to be okay. But it wasn't okay, he thought morosely, looking at the vegetation invading the damaged cockpit. Not by a long shot.

Deciding to leave Dr. Eve where she was, until he'd made sure they weren't about to slide tail-first into an active volcano, Chase pulled himself upright. The move brought him closer. Closer to the intoxicating scent of woman… closer to temptation.

He quickly lurched out of reach, telling himself it was a good thing he was over women like her.

A *real* good thing.

Eve surfaced slowly, aware of a gang of vindictive road workers using power drills inside her skull. She frowned and tried to shift away from the excavation, but the move sent pain stabbing through her.

Oh…ow! What…what the—?

Carefully drawing in a shallow breath, she took stock, wondering where she was, why she couldn't remember… and why the heck someone was sitting on her chest. Then something cold and damp touched her head, right where it hurt. She gave a distressed moan and lifted her hand to swat feebly at the annoyance.

"G'way," she mumbled crossly, shivering when a trickle of cold water made its way down her throat.

"Keep still," a deep, familiar voice ordered, sending a bolt of something that felt like panic through her body.

Her eyes and mouth flew open, with the intention of giving him a piece of her mind, but the words froze in her throat when she found the hunky sea god close. Very

close…and wet. As if she'd invaded his ocean kingdom
and he was holding her hostage.

Yikes.

Every thought promptly flew right out of her head.

It was like déjà vu.

Or more like déjà dead.

She moaned softly on realizing that every part of her
hurt. Even her eyes, which she narrowed against the light.

"Oh, great," she rasped hoarsely. "I should have known.
I'm dead, and the pilot from hell isn't done torturing me."

A spark of amusement briefly lit his storm-gray eyes,
along with a look of what couldn't possibly be concern and
wild relief. Could it? And why hadn't she noticed before
how long and thick his dark lashes were?

Annoyance replaced the amusement, momentarily dis-
tracting her from the wet cloth he pressed to her pounding
head. She tried evading it, but he gently cradled her head
and turned her toward him.

"Keep still," he muttered irritably. "I had to move you
before I could check for internal injuries."

"Isn't that *my* line?" she rasped, gasping when he hit a
particularly tender spot. *"Ouch!"* She grabbed his hand,
her fingers barely fitting around the brawny wrist as she
attempted to hold him off. And when she discovered that
all she could do was cling weakly as he carefully dabbed
the area, she grimaced.

Oh, yeah—and moaned. She could definitely moan too,
she discovered—the low sound was slipping out without
her permission. It was downright embarrassing. Besides,
she was the doctor, dammit. Wasn't it *her* job to heal the
injured?

"That…hurts…"

What didn't hurt was the oddly arousing sensation of
crisp hair against her sensitive palm. It was more like a life-
line to something solid and safe. Then she noticed something dark and wet matting his thick hair, the pallor beneath

his smoothly tanned skin, and her senses abruptly sharpened into medic mode.

With renewed determination she shoved his hand away and struggled into a sitting position, gasping and wheezing because her chest felt as if it was being crushed.

"What...what the heck have you done to me?" she rasped, wondering if this was what it felt like to have a coronary. If so, she suddenly had a wealth of sympathy for anyone who'd ever had one.

His startled, "Huh?" was followed by a growled, "I saved your ass, if that's what you mean..." accompanied by an injured scowl, as if she should be grateful that she ached everywhere. And she meant *everywhere*. "And just in case you forgot, *lady*, this is the second time in less than eight hours."

Eve ignored him and looked past his mile-wide shoulders and aggravated expression.

What she saw had her eyes widening in shock.

She gasped at the sight of the padded seats, twisted at odd angles, and the stuff strewn everywhere. There was also a large plastic sheet covering a jagged hole where the wall—fuselage?— used to be. Chase must have rigged it to block out the storm, but water still continued to pour in along the sides.

Then the truth dawned on her and her gaze snapped back to him, her mouth dropping open at the realization that they'd—

"Ohmigod, you crashed?"

Dull color crept up his neck and he snapped out an insulted, "I did no such thing. The storm—"

"We're upside down!" she interrupted, craning her head around his wide shoulders, slack-jawed as she studied the crazy angle of everything.

It made her feel off balance, because neither the floor nor the ceiling was where it should be.

Her gaze swung back to his, and when he opened his

mouth Eve sucked in a quick breath and accused, "You said everything was going to be okay."

A muscle twitched in his hard jaw and his expression darkened even more. "It *is*."

"You said you'd handle things."

"I *did*," he gritted out, his stormy gaze locking with hers so intently that Eve finally realized he wasn't as calm as she'd thought. And he looked…embarrassed, even.

They were barely hanging on to life and he was *embarrassed*? Typical alpha guy.

"How? In case you haven't noticed, you crashed your plane."

"No kidding?" he drawled, with a wealth of sarcasm that Eve thought was entirely unwarranted. "Congratulations, Miz Observant. In case *you* haven't figured it out, direct lightning strikes tend to fry electronics. So, yeah," he snarled, "we crashed. Happy?"

She sighed, recalling the sight of the seaplane, gleaming white and obviously well cared for as it bobbed gently on the bright blue waters of Port Laurent. "I'm sorry. It was a beautiful plane."

He grunted, looking even more dejected if that was possible.

She tried for a conciliatory tone. "Do you…um…know where we are?"

He was silent for a couple beats, then he flicked her a speculative glance, as though trying to decide how to tell her that they'd crashed on the back of a giant sea turtle—or maybe in the middle of a volcano.

"You mean other than in a wrecked plane?"

Something very close to panic edged its way into Eve's consciousness. He was looking at her with hooded gray eyes that had gone strangely wary. Conciliation went right out the window.

"You have no idea where we are, do you?"

"Well, not at the mo—"

"Oh. My. God." Her eyes widened and clung to his, in the vain hope that he was joking. "You don't!" she accused, the crushing feeling in her chest returning with a vengeance.

"Well, not *exactly*," he growled, flashing an unreadable glance in her direction. "But you're fine, aren't you? No broken bones or anything? Right?" He didn't even have the grace to look apologetic.

Eve's heart lurched into her throat, threatening to cut off her air. She gasped for breath and clutched at her chest, where her heart threatened to punch its way through her ribs.

She sucked in another painful breath. *This could not be happening.* She'd fallen asleep and was still having a nightmare about the South Pacific and a flyboy from hell. But that was okay. Any minute now she'd wake up and—

"Fine? You call this *fine*?" Her voice rose to a hysterical squeak. *"Oh, God."* Air whooshed in and out of her lungs a few times as she tried to calm herself, but she wasn't getting calmer—in fact her vision was graying at the edges. "I…think…I'm having…a heart attack."

"You're just hyperventilating," he said, with such masculine impatience she was tempted to whack him in the head. *Oh, wait.* He'd already been whacked in the head—which probably explained his abhorrent personality.

No, that wasn't true. He'd been like that before the crash.

"Take a deep breath before you faint again."

"I am *not* going to faint," she snapped, trying to calm her panicked breathing. *Oh, God, she was totally going to pass out.* "I just can't seem to…to take a deep…breath. My chest…feels…it feels like…you…punched…me."

"That's just bruising from the harness. Maybe you should let me check you out?" he offered helpfully. "Maybe you broke a few ribs."

"And maybe you should back the hell off," Eve wheezed,

slapping at the hand reaching out to help unbutton her silk blouse. "You just want to gawk at the goods."

Chase sat back with an exasperated huff. "Lady, I've already 'gawked at the goods,' as you so delicately put it," he announced.

When she narrowed her eyes on him, as though imagining taking a scalpel to his intestines, he gave a careless shrug. "If it makes you feel better, you're not my type. So I can be all professional without going insane with lust."

Eve growled, and when Chase ventured a glance at her face she was—*surprise, surprise*—glaring at him, her lush bottom lip caught between pearly white teeth.

He groaned silently. *Dammit*. Now was *not* the time to be noticing her mouth. She was mad. He was mad. And they both needed medical attention. And since she was the doctor—yeah, well, maybe he shouldn't think about her kissing anything better...

"But if you ask real nice..." he drawled, helping himself to a mouthful of bottled water and wishing it was expensive whiskey instead. Because, *man*, if there was ever a time for alcohol-induced mindlessness, it was now. "When we get outta here, I'll help you with that little problem you were screaming about earlier."

Large amber eyes blinked at him in confusion, and then he knew the instant she recalled what she'd been talking... *screaming*...about before they'd crashed. Her eyelashes flickered and her throat convulsed around an audible swallow. A faint blush crept into her cheeks.

Then her pink tongue sneaked out and slid over that bottom lip he was having such hot fantasies about and *he* was the one swallowing hard.

"Wh-what problem?" she rasped. "The only problem I have here is you." Her gaze slid around the interior of the cabin rather than look at him. "And the fact that you crashed your plane."

Ignoring her attempts to distract him, he held out the bottle and said, "Well…it was kinda hard to hear above all the hysteria, but I *think* you were babbling something about never having had a screaming orgasm."

She snatched the bottle on a strangled squeak of horror. "I most certainly did *not*." The blush had turned wild, staining her pale skin a rosy pink.

"You most certainly did," he said, enjoying himself enormously now that her attention had been diverted from his plane and her panic attack.

"Don't be ridiculous. I'm th-thirty. Of course I've had org—plenty of those."

He pointed at her. "See? You can't even say it." He swallowed a chuckle when she made a growling sound in her throat. "You're not my type, or anything, but I don't mind admitting it took everything I had just to concentrate on flying. Which, come to think of it, was probably why we crashed." His look turned accusatory. "So I guess it's *your* fault."

"You're…you're insane," she spluttered.

He hitched a shoulder. "Anyway, I thought…being fellow survivors and all…" He clenched his jaw on a chuckle at her expression and turned it into a cough. Her face was a mix of relief, outrage and stunned disbelief.

Priceless.

And almost worth crashing his baby.

Almost.

"Besides," he continued after clearing his throat, "not many guys get to be wrecked on a deserted tropical island with an exotic underwear model."

Her eyes widened and her fingers gave a convulsive jerk. Water shot up the plastic neck of the bottle, spilling all over her hand and down the front of her shirt. For about ten seconds she spluttered, her mouth opening and closing several times. She looked ready to toss the water in his face. Or maybe smack him on the head with it.

Considering he already had the mother of all headaches, he carefully edged out of reach.

"Better not waste that water," he warned, in case she gave in to temptation. "It's all we have."

Fighting the heat of embarrassment at being reminded of her temporary loss of control, Eve tugged nervously at her skirt and couldn't help thinking about the fact that she wasn't "his type."

Really? That's what you're focusing on?

"Lingerie," she said primly, wriggling around to pull at her narrow skirt. She didn't know why she cared. Let him look. There was absolutely no way she wanted this…this rude, obnoxious *heathen* thinking she was his type. Thinking that she *wanted* to be his type—even if she did get a hot flash every time his gaze dropped to her legs.

She didn't. Not even if he were the last man on earth.

"Huh?" The heathen gave her an odd look and she wondered for a mortifying moment if she'd spoken out loud.

"Lingerie—not underwear. Men wear underwear. There's a difference."

"Hmm…" he murmured, squinting at her chest as though he could see through her blouse.

She quickly glanced down and gave a sigh of relief when she saw that he couldn't.

"So you *do* model lingerie?"

Of course he knew she didn't. He was just baiting her. *The jerk*.

"Of course not," Eve snapped, rising irritably to the bait, anyway. "What gave you that idea?"

"You did."

"I think you hit your head," she said, eyeing his bruised, battered face and the wet gleam of blood matting his dark hair with sudden concern. But despite the obvious pain around his eyes he looked… *Oh, boy!* He looked good. Like an irreverent, roughed-up pirate, ready to raise hell.

Her belly quivered. A really *hot* hell-raising pirate, darn it.

His mouth quirked, as though he knew what she was thinking. "Maybe you should let me check it out for myself. For educational purposes, of course," he added innocently when she gave a muffled growl. "To show me the difference between lingerie and underwear."

Seeing the wicked gleam, she narrowed her eyes to dangerous slits. "You. Are. Evil," she said through clenched teeth, and shifted farther away from him—which wasn't far enough, given their cramped quarters. "And instead of focusing on my underwear you should be thinking about where we are and…and…" She sucked in a shaky breath as their situation hit her. "Oh, God, how we're going to be rescued."

He sent her a dirty look, as if she'd insulted his manhood, and gingerly lay down on the pile of towels he'd used to make a pallet. When he said nothing—even closed his eyes—Eve wondered if his head injury had affected his memory.

Fear crawled into her belly like a sly fox invading a chicken coop.

"What about the radio? Did you try the radio?"

He sighed. "Of *course* I tried the radio," he muttered irritably, without opening his eyes. "It's fried—like the rest of the electronics. And before you nag me about where we are, and how we're going to be rescued, all I can say is I don't know." His lids popped open and his dark eyes settled on her, oddly serious and hypnotic. "I checked earlier and all I can see is jungle. We crashed in a damn jungle." He sighed again. "But better than the sea, huh?"

After a short silence, during which she had no clue how to reply to such male logic, his expression lightened and he gave her an up-and-down look that lingered a little too long on her breasts.

"So," he said, deliberately changing the subject. "You're a GP?"

"No, I'm an OB-GYN."

"OB what?"

"OB-GYN. I specialize in pregnancy, birth and women's…um…reproduction organs."

He absorbed that silently while Eve felt the heat rise in her cheeks. She was a medical professional, for heaven's sake. There was absolutely no need to blush at the mention of reproduction and childbirth.

It was normal. Completely natural.

So why did it suddenly seem intimate and…and slightly indecent, discussing it with him?

"And you've *never* been a lingerie model?"

"No," she said with strained patience. "I've never been *any* kind of model. I've waited tables, cleaned motel rooms, and I did a stint at a doughnut shop and then a…" She stopped before she admitted that she'd also worked in an exclusive boutique, which was where she'd got her love of expensive lingerie. She could just imagine his reaction to *that*. "Well, never mind. Suffice it to say I've never had the slightest desire to parade around in my underwear."

With a little smile tugging the corner of his mouth, he studied her until her face grew hot. "Huh."

"What?"

He grunted an incomprehensible reply and returned his gaze somewhere over her head, as though disappointed by her answer. "I had this roomate in college who was specializing in gynecology," he admitted after a short silence. "He was this huge bear of a guy who couldn't ever seem to find clean socks, let alone know which end a baby was supposed to emerge from. You're nothing like him."

Unsure whether or not to be insulted, Eve rolled her eyes. "You went to college?" And then she could have kicked herself when his eyebrow rose up his forehead. She hadn't meant to sound insulting.

At least she didn't think so.

"Oh, yeah," he said sleepily, and Eve leaned closer to study the gash on his head. "Even managed to get a degree and everything."

"In what?" she murmured absently, more worried about his slurred speech and his pallor than the amount of blood.

"How to raise hell while charming a girl out of her underwear?"

He chuckled tiredly. "Lingerie," he murmured, closing his eyes.

"What?"

"It's lingerie, remember?" And when she continued to stare at him in confusion he slurred, "You said so yourself. Men wear underwear."

Ignoring his babbling, she shook her head and focused on the important details. "If you have a degree, what are you doing flying tourists around the South Pacific in a flying boat?"

He tilted his head toward her and cracked open one laser-sharp gray eye. After a while he said, "It's a long, boring story."

When she just continued to look at him, he shrugged and shut his eye again.

"If you must know…"

He yawned, and Eve found herself holding her breath as if he was about to impart state secrets.

She had to lean forward to hear his murmured, "Keeps me in mai tais."

Her breath whooshed out in what she told herself *wasn't* disappointment, and she sat back to nibble uncertainly on her lip while considering what his head injury might mean. First, he was the only thing between her and an unknown, possibly hostile jungle. And second, despite the weird things those mocking gray eyes did to her control—like unravel it faster than line on a fishing reel—being in a jungle with a head injury was the last thing anyone wanted.

"I…um…" She cleared her throat and tucked her hair behind her ear. "I don't think you should close your eyes."

"I'm tired, and my head hurts like a bi— It hurts." He grunted, and she nearly smiled at his obvious attempt to clean up his language. "Hell, *everything* hurts."

She could sympathize. She was feeling every bruise, along with an adrenaline crash, and was all too willing to sink into a healing sleep herself. "I mean, I really don't think you should sleep."

Something in her tone must have registered, because his eyes popped open and he frowned at her. He sat up abruptly and looked around, as if he expected a horde of savages to be hiding behind the seats. "Why? What's wrong?"

"You have a head injury and you might be concussed."

"You have a head injury too," he pointed out reasonably, waving a hand in her direction, and she was somewhat taken aback that the mention of her head suddenly had it pounding like a heavy metal band.

"But…but I'm not concussed," she reasoned, fairly certain she wasn't—although she did have a splitting headache. Probably nothing a couple of painkillers and a bottle of water wouldn't fix. Oh, yeah, and about twelve hours' sleep.

"How do you know?" he demanded, sinking back onto the mound of towels with a groan. "You were out for a long time."

She digested that piece of information. "How long?"

"I don't know. A while."

Which meant he'd also been unconscious.

She looked around the cabin at the scattered debris. "Do you have a first-aid box?"

His mouth quirked, drawing her attention to the finely sculpted lips that did odd things to her insides. But then again it had been hours since she'd eaten, so she was probably just hungry.

"Strapped to the bulkhead behind you." He waited for

her to retrieve it before asking innocently, "We gonna play doctor, Doctor?"

She raised her eyebrows at him and opened the box, surprised to find it fully stocked with top-of-the-range supplies. More than adequate for a minor emergency—maybe even minor surgery.

"No," she said absently, mulling over another piece of the puzzle that was Chase Gallagher—the fact that he'd spared no expense on the seaplane he used to keep him in mai tais. "I'm going to do what I've been trained for."

She removed packaged swabs, antiseptic spray and some packaged adhesive strips from the steel box and placed them beside her.

"Should I be worried?"

Her gaze shot up and caught his smirk. "Worried?" she asked warily, not knowing how to handle him in his current mood. Scowling and cursing were easier to handle than this…this teasing and dangerously attractive man. Maybe the whack on the head had changed his personality. Or, worse, maybe the whack on *her* head had rendered her temporarily insane. "I'm an excellent doctor."

"A skull fracture is a far cry from childbirth and 'women's…um…reproduction organs,'" he said, perfectly mimicking her earlier words.

Her eyes narrowed and she contemplated doing a lobotomy on him, to take care of that personality change. "I wouldn't worry, if I were you," she drawled smoothly. "It's just big and hard."

The instant the words were out of her mouth she wished them back—especially when the wicked gleam turned to outright laughter. She sent him a dirty look that made him laugh even more, until she slapped a wad of alcohol swabs on his head.

Sucking in a sharp breath, he grabbed her wrist and eyed her warily. "Are you sure you're a doctor? You blush at the mention of reproduction and your bedside manner sucks."

"Newborns and their mothers are perfectly safe with me," she snapped. "It's just the *big* babies that need to watch out."

His mouth curled into a half-assed grin that she shouldn't have found appealing. *Oh, wow.*

"You're calling me a big baby?"

She shrugged, and a strange sensation moved through her at the sudden image of him as a little boy, his usually wicked gray eyes filled with hurt as his mother kissed his boo-boos.

Then he snorted derisively and she decided he'd probably emerged fully grown—with a sexy scowl.

Darn.

Now she was visualizing him wearing nothing *but* that sexy scowl.

A sigh escaped. She was obviously in need of medical attention herself if she was finding him—his *scowl*—sexy.

"Are you flirting with me, Dr. Carmichael?"

She rolled her eyes, and instantly regretted the move when pain stabbed behind her right eye, reminding her that she'd hit her head sometime during the crash—and also against his when they'd collided earlier. *Yeesh.* Maybe her injury was worse than she'd thought. A serious injury was the only explanation for imagining this…this sexy heathen as a vulnerable little boy. And then getting all mushy about it.

"Don't be ridiculous," she muttered, ducking her head and sliding her hands through his damp hair so she could examine his injury.

You were so flirting. The knowledge had her nipples tightening and her belly quivering with alarm, along with a renewed determination to ignore his bad-boy allure. She was *nothing* like her mother. *Nothing.* She'd hardly had a string of wild hookups that had resulted in not one but two unwanted pregnancies, along with heartbreak, cleared-out bank accounts and a few bruises. Besides, she'd worked since she was about thirteen and hadn't had the time.

"This is hardly the time or place."

There will be no time or place, Evelyn, she reminded herself firmly. *Bad boys are bad. Period.*

"You have something better to do?"

She sent him a long cool look. "You mean like checking for oozing brain matter?" She reached for more swabs. "I'd say there's little chance of that, Mr. Gallagher. You appear to have lost all yours."

CHAPTER FOUR

OH, YEAH, CHASE thought moodily. He clearly *had* lost brain cells if the sensation of her fingers sliding though his hair was suddenly the most erotic thing he'd ever experienced.

He sighed, closed his eyes. *Great. Just freaking great.* Not only had he lost his plane, his mind had taken a hike too. The former was insured, but the latter... Well, he didn't know which one he'd miss the most.

He'd thought closing his eyes would shut her out, but he hadn't figured on the sensation of her fingers in his hair, or the heat and scent of her body invading his nostrils as she leaned close.

He found himself focusing on drawing in her wildly erotic scent and thought, *Aw, man, just my luck to want to jump Amelia's sister.* Which was not only wrong but strange, considering he'd never felt a lick of attraction for his future sister-in-law. But he wanted to yank Eve down, roll her beneath him and ravish her smart mouth.

She nibbled on a plump pink lip and he sucked in a sharp breath. Her forehead wrinkled at the sound, and when she dropped her gaze to his, they both froze.

The air sizzled and Chase's pulse leaped into an abrupt gallop. The next moment a crushing weight descended on his chest as the air inside the plane seemed to be sucked out. There one instant, then...*vhoop*...gone.

The moment stretched out and with each thundering

beat of his heart her pupils grew, until only a thin circle of shimmering amber remained. His skin hummed, his ears buzzed and all he could think about was letting himself drown in deepest, darkest velvet.

Before he realized what he was doing, he wrapped his fingers in her silk shirt and yanked her down. Instead of putting his mouth on her, like he wanted, swallowing her in one big, greedy gulp, he paused, holding her mouth barely a breath away from his.

She gave a strangled gasp.

His scalp literally crawled with the instinct to cover her mouth with his and swallow that soft sound—and any others she made. Along with more. A whole hell of a lot more.

For several long moments they remained frozen, eyes locked and mouths almost touching, floating in a silent world that contained nothing but heat, ragged breathing and a startling savage hunger.

Finally Chase realized that her huge eyes were dilated with wariness as much as with arousal. His gut clenched and his fingers tightened. *Dammit*, what the hell was wrong with him? He didn't usually grab women and practically force his kisses on them.

With a sound of disgust—mainly at himself—he gently nudged her backward, widening the gap between them. And hopefully removing temptation.

His jaw ached along with the rest of his body.

Looking a little shell-shocked, Evelyn lifted unsteady fingers to her mouth. She blinked at him, and then away, her breath as unsteady as his. He wanted to curse himself for putting that wary look in her eyes. Then again, better wariness than the hot, dark need that was a lit match to his.

She opened her mouth, then shut it again, her brow wrinkling in irritation as much as confusion.

"What the hell was that?" she rasped, sounding as if she'd chewed on glass.

He grunted out a mirthless laugh. "Damned if I know."

And when he felt his neck heat he rolled onto his side, presenting her with his back.

After a lengthy silence, she cleared her throat. "I'm not finished dressing your head wound," she said briskly, but Chase could feel her eyes boring holes in his back.

"I'm fine," he muttered.

He would not apologize. It was her fault, anyway. For looking at him with those shimmering eyes. Yeah, and nibbling on that plump lip. He was a guy who'd been on the sex wagon for a while. She was smart. She should know better than to tempt a starving man.

"If I need any doctoring," he practically snarled, "I'll let you know. Right now I'm tired. So...good night."

There was a moment of stunned silence, then Chase heard her moving around, muttering to herself about giving grumpy flyboys a lobotomy to improve their personalities.

But his personality was fine. Or it had been until she'd swooned into his life. Maybe it was *her* attitude that needed adjusting. Didn't she know that men were attracted to soft, feminine women? Women who didn't hike their eyebrows and look at a man like he was a delinquent in need of disciplining. Women who didn't treat a man as if he was a moron for crashing his seaplane.

He snorted silently. If that was true, then why the hell did he find her smart mouth and sharp wit so darn...*sexy*?

Heart hammering, Eve gaped at the ragged path Chase's seaplane had cleared through the jungle before coming to rest at a drunken angle about fifty yards in. One wing and a pontoon had broken right off, leaving the bulk of the battered plane half-buried in thick tropical vegetation and tilted at an impossible angle.

The sight had her sucking in air and locking her knees against the urge to sink to the ground.

How did I not feel this happening?
How did we manage to walk away from this?

The last thing she remembered was the seaplane flipping upside down and a scream tearing from her throat. She'd been convinced she was going to die.

And then… She inhaled and exhaled noisily, until her heart rate settled and the black dots swimming behind her eyes disappeared. Then she recalled waking up to a wet, half-naked sea god bending over her—for the second time in less than twelve hours.

The whole thing seemed…surreal, somehow. As though it had happened to someone else. As though she'd opened her eyes to find herself in someone else's nightmare.

This morning she'd woken to the sounds of shrieks and squawks, convinced that hostile animals had invaded her bedroom. But she'd been in a wrecked seaplane.

Nowhere near the sea.

For a long moment she'd lain absolutely still, absorbing the shock, because she'd kind of hoped that it had all been a bad dream.

No such luck.

Now, smoothing the hair off her face with trembling fingers, Eve looked everywhere but at the crumpled plane. It was past dawn and the sky—what she could see of it—was lavender and a wild orange-red that reminded her of that childhood saying about a red sky in the morning being a sailor's warning.

She gave a soft snort. It would have been *really* great if she'd had that warning yesterday morning, on her stopover at Oahu. Maybe she would have been prepared for the coming disaster. Maybe she could have avoided it altogether by turning around and heading back to London.

She let out a sigh and looked around.

Speaking of disasters…where the heck was Chase?

For a couple of really intense moments she'd thought he'd ditched her, but then she'd remembered how he'd treated her the night before. Impatience mixed with baffled tenderness. It had been a novel, if uncomfortable experience. Especially as she'd always had to be the strong one. For her mother, her grandmother…Amelia. It had been kind of nice to let someone else be strong for once.

Just briefly, she reminded herself quickly. Because life had taught her that she couldn't rely on people. When she did, they either left or died on her.

After the heat and intensity of that weird almost-kiss she'd escaped outside, hoping to get her emotions under control before she faced him again. But she needn't have worried. By the time she'd returned he was fast asleep. With nothing to do, she'd swallowed a couple of pain meds and stretched out beside him—and had been asleep within minutes.

She'd woken once, to find herself snuggled against a large warm body as though she'd sought his heat, and when she'd bolted upright—*horrified*—he'd muttered irritably and tugged her back down, yanking her against him.

They'd had a brief tug-of-war that he'd won by throwing one heavy leg over her and growling at her to go to sleep. She'd finally succumbed, wrapped in delicious heat and feeling strangely relaxed and contented.

If she hadn't been so exhausted she might have had the presence of mind to freak out. Or maybe slip from his embrace. But she hadn't. And she hadn't been disappointed when she'd awakened to find herself alone either.

Well, not much.

Keeping a sharp lookout for snakes and spiders—because *everyone* knew there were serpents, even of the two-legged variety, in paradise—she took care of her morning business before setting off toward the beach. She bravely ignored all the strange rustling coming from the dense undergrowth and hurried as fast as her bare feet and stiff muscles could carry her.

She was acutely aware of the ridiculous picture she must make, picking her way through broken branches, jagged plant stems and squishy ground cover dressed in a rumpled

green pencil skirt and a cream silk blouse, clutching a pair
of strappy high heels.

With all her scrapes and bruises, she probably looked
like an advertisement for domestic abuse.

Or—*yikes*—the morning after a *very* rough night before.

She rolled her eyes. So much for her professional image,
she thought—which, come to think of it, had tanked just
about the time she'd landed in paradise.

And met him, of course.

He was clearly bad luck. And she was done with bad
luck. *Soooo done*. From now on her life was going to be
charmed. Or she'd have something to say about it.

By the time she emerged from the trees to step onto soft,
cool sand, tinted pink in the early-morning light and lit-
tered with storm debris, Eve was huffing, perspiring and
wondering when the heck she'd let herself get so out of
shape. Although it might have something to do with the
dark bruises across her chest and belly, or the many hours
since her last decent meal.

Thinking about food made her stomach growl, although she'd rather have a long hot soak in scented bubbles.
Scented bubbles up to her neck, surrounded by candles, a
bottle of wine. Oh…and a hot bronzed sea god to massage
her aching body.

Inhaling the amazingly cool and fresh morning air, she
looked up—and promptly froze. Because the sea god had
stepped out of her vision into the flesh— She blinked. He
was emerging from the turquoise water. Her eyes widened.
He was…he was…*naked*.

Ohmigod! He *so* was naked. Her breath escaped in a
stuttered whoosh. Gloriously naked. From the top of his
seal-dark wet hair to his big tanned feet and everything—
she meant *everything*—in between. And—she gulped—
there certainly was a *lot* of "in-between."

She must have made a sound, because he stopped shaking water from his hair and lifted his head, stormy eyes zeroing in on her with laser-point accuracy.

Eve's gaze flew upward and her mind came to a screeching halt.

For a long, breathless moment they stared at each other, the memory of last night like a blaze across the fifteen feet separating them. Finally an arrogant dark brow rose up his bruised forehead, galvanizing Eve into action.

She squeaked out an *"Oh!"* slapped a hand over her eyes in delayed reaction and half spun away, aware that her entire body had gone hot because she'd been caught eyeing his package. The image had been burned onto her retina—her brain—for all time.

An amused baritone drawled, "Enjoying the view?" and Eve could have kicked herself for reacting like a ninth grader caught in the boys' locker room.

"What—what the heck are you d-doing?" she squeaked, stalling for time. She peeked at him through the gaps in her fingers and admired—professionally, of course—the wide shoulders, the clearly defined but not overly bulky deltoids, biceps, pectorals, the eight-...*eight?*...pack and the deep vee arrowing down to—

"Taking an early-morning swim." He interrupted her awestruck mental anatomy list, scooping up his shirt with which he proceeded to dry himself off—totally unconcerned with his nudity.

She squeezed her eyes closed and waved her hand in his direction, thinking if she looked like that she'd probably be unconcerned too. Because...

Whoa.

"But you're..." She snapped her mouth shut at the sudden realization that she was acting like a scandalized old maid and not a medical practitioner who'd seen her share of naked bodies. "I mean your head. You're, um...concussed."

He snorted, as though he knew she hadn't been referring to his head injury. "It's fine. In fact I feel great."

Well, he certainly *looked* great. And would probably feel great too. Especially if she—

There was a rustle of fabric and then his amused voice drawled, "It's safe now, Dr. Prim. You can look."

Eve's eyes snapped open to find him barely a foot away, looking all cool and damp and...and *amused*, darn him. But *safe* was hardly a word she'd use in connection with this sexy, grumpy pilot. Especially on a storm-ravaged beach with that dark, dangerous aura surrounding his half-naked form and making him look like he belonged in this wild, deserted place.

Then she looked closer and caught the way he held himself, held his head and shoulders. Stiffly and carefully—as though it hurt to move.

"You're lying," she accused, relieved to be reminded of her profession. Relieved because now she could focus on something other than all that masculine awesomeness.

Stepping closer, she reached up to cup his head so she could examine his eyes. He froze, as though her touch surprised him, and for a moment it surprised her too. But then she told herself that they'd survived a terrifying ordeal and even slept together. What she was doing was in a professional capacity, and not...definitely *not* because of a sudden overwhelming need to touch him.

He looked tired, she thought, and he was trying to hide his pain. Her sigh was an exhalation of exasperation. Men made really sucky patients—which was one of the reasons she'd gone into obstetrics and gynecology.

The other had been personal. Her grandmother, Isadora, had been a midwife, and Eve had often been called on to help. Sometimes, like the night her mother had died giving birth to her second set of twins, things had gone bad, and the remembered helplessness had motivated her in the long, hard years of studying medicine and holding down three jobs.

She held up three fingers.

"How many?"

His hooded gaze remained locked on hers and Eve's heart gave a funny little stutter in her chest at the smoldering intensity turning his gray eyes smoky. He wrapped a large hand around hers, trapping her fingers in warmth. The little stutter became a wild tumble that she felt clear to the soles of her feet. The next thing she knew her nipples had tightened into painful points.

Her knees wobbled. She sucked in a shocked breath and her mouth promptly went dry. That had been…unexpected, to say the least. And totally unwelcome, she told herself firmly, nervously sliding her tongue over her bottom lip as she tried to tug her hand free. His grip was gentle, unbreakable, and short of an embarrassing tussle, she wasn't going anywhere.

His thumb set up a hypnotizing caress. "If I tell you where it hurts," he murmured, his gaze dropping to her mouth, "will you kiss it better?"

Her stunned "What…?" ended in a muffled *oomph* when he used his possession of her hand to yank her against him. Right up against that awesome naked chest covered in bruises.

"How 'bout we start here?" he growled roughly, and before Eve could react he swooped down and closed his mouth over hers.

Her eyes widened in shock. There was nothing tentative or gentle about the move. In fact if she'd had the ability to think she might have said it was forceful and more than a little heated. As though he'd been compelled to give in to some wild, dark impulse and blamed her for it.

She made a soft sound of protest, which he promptly swallowed, and when she tried to jerk away, his hands speared into her hair, wrapping around her head to hold her captive as he set about totally overpowering her senses. He didn't ask permission or even coax. He just *took*, blasting through her defenses with his mouth and tongue, consuming all thoughts of resistance along with her breath.

Dizzy, Eve clutched at the nearest surface and found smooth, warm masculine flesh beneath her hands. But that was okay. More than okay, actually.

In the guise of needing something solid to hold on to, she did what she *really* wanted to do.

It took her hands only a few seconds to explore his abdomen, glorying in the way the steely muscles twitched and rippled beneath her touch. And then she became lost in the mindless haze of his kisses, unaware that she was greedily and possessively exploring acres of smooth warm flesh with her hands while her mouth answered the demand of his.

She'd never experienced anything remotely like it. He sucked her in like a level-five twister, until she sagged against him, all control over her limbs forgotten.

One arm snaked around her waist, anchoring her against him as he whipped her up and sent her senses spinning into an endless moment of shocking heat and erotic need. A need she'd never before experienced.

The kiss seemed to last forever, and when he finally released her mouth to suck in air, she wheezed, "That's… that's not how you k-kiss anything…um…better." She was shocked that anything remotely coherent had emerged from her mouth. Even more shocked that the mere touch of a man's mouth could leave her feeling so…*changed*.

His dark brow rose up his forehead and his eyes glittered with humor—and something imminently incendiary—as though no one had dared question his technique before.

But, Eve noted with satisfaction, his heart was pounding beneath her hand…the hand currently smoothing over hard pectoral muscles covered in warm taut skin. The other was curled into the waistband of his cargoes, against taut, satiny-smooth skin—as if she'd needed to hold on to something or risk falling at his feet like a boneless blob.

"Oh, yeah?"

"No," she said, wondering why she wasn't getting as far away from him as possible.

She didn't even like him, for heaven's sake, and that kiss couldn't have been further from her idea of romantic than if he'd hauled back and slugged her. It had been too intense—an assault on her senses. It had left her breathless, dazed, which might have something to do with the fact that when she moved her hand just a fraction to the left she abruptly froze when she realized exactly what she was touching.

Oh, boy. It looked like he'd dressed in a hurry and forgotten his underwear.

Her breath hitched and her senses swam—which was probably why she did what she did next.

Sliding her free hand up to cup his jaw, she eased up the length of his body on her toes and pressed against this evidence of his reaction to their little experiment.

"*This* is how you do it," she murmured huskily, and with her eyes locked on his she very carefully touched her mouth to the heavy bruise on his shoulder, before moving to his jaw, covered in a sexy two-day stubble and a dark bruise. The delicious rasp against her lips sent a shudder of pure sensation racing over her flesh, making her skin prickle and each tiny hair lift…as if straining to be closer still.

Her lips curved against his jaw and his hands, warm and heavy at her hips, clenched almost convulsively, as though he fought the need to crush her against him.

The heat in his now-stormy eyes blazed hot and bright. Her belly clenched with nerves and something that felt very much like…excitement?

No. Her eyelids fluttered and she froze. *No getting excited, Evelyn. This isn't some adolescent make-out session that you can control or laugh off.*

He was a fully grown man, with over a foot and a hundred pounds on her. There was no controlling *him*—or the way he made her body react.

Her breath shuddered out against his skin and he turned his head. A sound—deep and rough and thrilling—emerged from his throat. "Don't stop there," he growled softly, his sculpted lips brushing hers and making them tingle.

Oh, yeah. Definitely time to stop.

"I…um…" She slid her hands to his shoulders and tried to ease away, but his grip on her hips tightened, holding her firmly against him. Right there, against all that delicious…um…hardness.

She sucked in a sharp breath, going still. The scent of warm aroused man had her eyes literally rolling back in her head. Suddenly the sheer size of him had her fighting two opposing instincts. One was to press closer and offer her mouth—heck, offer *everything*—the other…to escape.

She knew instinctively which one she should choose.

As though he knew what she was thinking Chase gave a low chuckle, the sound rumbling through his chest and sending delicious vibrations rolling through her body.

"Chicken, Doc?"

She swallowed. "D-don't be ridiculous." *More like terrified.* "I…I just think the lesson is over, that's all," she croaked, wedging her hands between their bodies and sucking in a shaky breath when her palms accidentally rasped against his tight male nipples. "I can see you're all better now."

"Liar," he crooned, shifting his hips closer, so the part he pressed against her belly was big and hard and… Eve's breath whooshed out.

And nothing.

Not feeling a thing here.

Her eyes widened. And not *there* either.

"I'm now in pain somewhere else," he murmured against her ear. "Wanna know where?"

Her gasp of outrage was muffled by his soft laughter and he allowed her to shove him away.

"You…you…" she stuttered, wanting to kick herself for rising to his bait. *"Jerk."* Wanting to kick *him* for making it so darn tempting.

"I meant my elbow," he said mildly, folding his arms across his wide chest and exposing another bruise. His eyebrow rose. "What did you *think* I meant?" The move made his biceps and deltoids bulge in a way that almost had her drooling.

No. No drooling.

And no touching after that last comment either.

"Besides, isn't a kiss supposed to cure everything?" he continued, when it was clear she wasn't going to reply.

"No," she snapped, tucking her hands into her armpits before they ignored her brain. "Not everything."

Not anything.

Because now she was in pain too. The kind of pain she'd read about but never experienced. The kind of pain she'd give anything not to feel. Certainly not with him.

"Uh-huh?" He sounded skeptical.

"Well, for one thing," she muttered, massaging the ache in her temple, "it won't cure your enormous ego."

He laughed and bent to pick up his damp shirt, which he held out to her with such a wicked look that her clothes nearly melted right off her body.

Deeply suspicious, she stared at it as though it might bite her, because it suddenly reminded her of the apple incident in the Garden of Eden. *Yeah, and look how that turned out.*

"What's that for?"

"I thought you might like a quick swim."

Instantly a vision of him joining her in the cool, clear water popped front and center into her head. A renewed surge of heat stained her cheeks—and blazed elsewhere when she realized that in her vision they were both naked and wet as seals.

She took a stumbling step backward, her hand flying up

to clutch the lapels of her blouse as though she was afraid he might offer to help her strip.

"But...but...shouldn't we be finding a way to get off this island?"

He shook his head as if she was hopeless and tossed his shirt at her. She barely caught it before it smacked her in the face.

"Doc, Doc, Doc..." He sighed, gesturing with his hand. "How often does anyone wake up to *this*? Besides," he added when she opened her mouth to argue, "I'm hungry. I'm going to find food. Go enjoy your swim. I promise not to peek."

Eve held the shirt to her front, as though it would provide an adequate shield against him. Against all that smooth, warm masculine skin. Against the urge to invite him to join her.

She pressed her lips together and he grinned before turning to head up the beach. "Suit yourself. Water's great, by the way," he called over his shoulder. "Might even cool you down."

Hah! As if.

Eve watched him disappear and thought it unlikely—especially as somewhere in the center of her body a fire raged, heating her up from the inside out.

It would take a lot to douse that.

Eve turned and eyed the crystal-clear water with sudden longing. It had been a couple of days since she'd taken more than a quick shower. Surely it wouldn't hurt to face the prospect of them being stranded on a deserted island, fresh and alert?

Casting around for a safe place to strip, she spied a secluded area and headed over to it. *Hmm*... She thoughtfully studied the area between some rock outcroppings. It made a perfect little cove, sheltered on both sides.

She cast a quick look over her shoulder at the empty beach and the line of thick jungle vegetation. Maybe if she undressed behind the rocks and slipped into the water there she wouldn't be seen. And if she saw someone coming—*fine, saw him coming*—she'd be able to scramble out and dress before he saw her.

Maybe.

She struggled mentally for about three seconds, before tossing his shirt onto the sand and quickly stripping out of her skirt and blouse. She was just about to wade into the water when she impulsively reached behind her to unfasten her bra. Before she could change her mind she shed it, along with the tiny matching cream and green lace panties, and added them to the growing pile.

Naked, Eve quickly waded into the water, her heart hammering at her daring. But then the water hit her midthigh and—*oh, God*—it felt amazing.

For just a moment her recent application for a new job in DC, her plans to start a new life there, seemed a million light years away. For just an instant she wondered what it must be like to live in this Garden of Eden, where life was simple.

Then she shook off her fanciful thoughts. Life was never simple, and this was nothing more than an amazing interlude. A harmless fantasy just like she and Amelia used to have as children.

And if the big male figure in her childhood fantasies had been replaced by someone infinitely more real—and more dangerous—she shrugged it off as delayed shock from surviving an air crash.

Her world, her life, was back in the States. All she had to do was find a way back to it.

CHAPTER FIVE

CHASE WENT OFF in search of food. He found bananas, a few small ripe papaya and some goji berries, and was wrapping his find in a banana leaf when an ear-piercing scream shattered the peace. The echo of it had barely registered when Chase dropped his bounty and tore through the vegetation toward the beach.

Damn, damn, *damn*. He shouldn't have left her alone. He should have ignored his promise not to look. He should have stayed…stood guard, done something. But, no. He had to go and make a stupid promise and now—*oh, God*—was she being attacked by a shark? Stung by box jellyfish? Or, worse, kidnapped by pirates?

Exploding onto the beach with a blood-curdling yell, he plowed to a halt in a shower of wet sand at the sight of the scene before him. His mouth dropped open more in shock than in an effort to fill his lungs with air after that mad dash.

A naked Eve—*and, boy, was that ironic*—stood with her back to him, facing the tiny cove and clutching his shirt to her front. He was momentarily distracted by the sight of her long slender back, heart-shaped bottom and endless Vegas showgirl legs before he realized she was facing a boatload of locals, all gaping at her as though she'd just been beamed down from the mothership.

The instant they saw him their attention swung his way,

and for a couple of beats they all seemed frozen in a tab-
leau that might have been comical if not for the fact that
his heart was pounding and his breath was sawing in an
out of his lungs.

Relieved that there wasn't a drop of blood in sight, he
lifted his arm in greeting, realizing that they hadn't crashed
onto a deserted island at all. And that she hadn't opened
an artery and didn't require CPR…although he probably
wouldn't have minded *that* so much.

Ambling down to the water's edge, Chase spied some
pieces of frothy lace that resembled sea foam and paused
to scoop them up. He shoved them into his pocket before
rescuing her blouse and skirt.

Eve must have sensed him behind her, and she cast a
wide-eyed, panic-filled glance over her shoulder as though
she expected a rear attack. When she saw him eyeing her
naked rear, she gave a distressed bleat and slapped a hand
over her bottom.

Covering absolutely nothing.

He arched a brow at her and held out her clothes, which
she snatched as she scurried crab-like behind him, careful not to flash her very excellent rear at the newcomers.

Using his body as a shield, she wheezed out, "Ohmigod,
ohmigod, ohmigod! Some protector you are. How *could
you*?"

Confused about why she was mad at *him*, he said,
"Huh?" and tried to turn around. But she squealed and
whacked his shoulder. He shook his head and faced forward. *Women.*

A couple men had hopped into the shallow water and
were pulling the boat closer to shore. Chase took a step
forward to help but was abruptly stopped when she curled
a hand into his waistband and yanked him back, growling,
"Move one inch and die," in his ear.

He might have laughed if the feel of her knuckles pressing into the small of his back hadn't threatened to blow the

top of his head right off. Goose bumps broke out across his skin and a shudder of pure lust zinged in all directions, turning him into one big electromagnetic generator. Or some kind of generator. Because he was suddenly harder than he'd ever been in his life. A breath away from ravishing Eve in paradise.

In clear view of a curious audience.

Shocked by the force of his reaction, he stuttered, "Wha-at?" wondering if the crash had caused permanent brain damage after all.

"Where the hell is my underwear?" she hissed from behind him, and Chase tried not to imagine her struggling to put on silk over wet skin. Wet naked skin.

His mouth curved with appreciation.

"Really?" he demanded out the corner of his mouth. "You're going to worry about that *now*?"

"What—what do you mean?"

He snorted and folded his arms across his chest. "What do you think I mean? This is a remote South Pacific island. You have to be on the lookout for pirates and human traffickers."

"Wha-a-a-at?" she squeaked behind him, and he nearly laughed at her gullibility.

But she'd cleaved herself to his back as though trying to get inside his skin. Instantly his entire being perked up, every hair covering his body standing straight up and saluting the sun. He promptly lost his train of thought.

And, *dammit*, his body hair wasn't the only thing saluting the sun.

He sucked in a shuddery breath. *Not now, Gallagher. Not ever. Not with her.*

"Chase Gallagher, is that you?"

Chase blinked to uncross his eyes and spotted Teiki Manea, a teacher whose wife had nearly lost her baby in the last stages of pregnancy a year ago. Chase had just dropped off a couple of tourists when Teiki had arrived, looking like a wild man, threatening to sink Chase's plane unless he flew them to the hospital in Rikirua.

Chase lifted his hands in a gesture of surrender. "Teiki? Don't tell me your wife's in labor again?"

The islander gave a booming laugh and charged up the beach to wrap his big arms around Chase. Chase returned the back slap—which was more of a pounding—and decided things could be worse. A lot worse.

The big islander's grin was quick and white. "And what if she is, *mon ami*?"

Chase shrugged. "The storm managed what you couldn't. My plane's wrecked."

"That was you?" Teiki demanded, stepping back to study the bruised and battered duo. "We heard something during the storm last night but—"

"Hey, don't sweat," Chase interrupted, knowing full well that a search party would have been dispatched immediately if it had been possible. "We're both fine."

Teiki snorted and peered around Chase to where Eve was zipping up her skirt. "You're uglier than ever," he said, smiling charmingly at Eve. "But your lady sure is fine."

Chase shook his head and laughed. He was about to tell Teiki that Eve wasn't his lady when she stepped around him and aimed a blinding smile at the islander. A smile that literally stole Chase's breath—along with his damn amusement.

What the—?

He gaped at her, captivated by the genuine laughter that transformed her from attractive to, well…stunning. And then, abruptly realizing he was standing there with his mouth hanging open, Chase snapped it shut and scowled at the way she beamed at Teiki—as though he'd just saved her from a fate worse than death.

So what the hell was Chase? Fish fungus?

"Teiki, this is Dr. Carmichael from the US." He practically bit out each word and folded his arms across his chest in case he gave in to the primitive impulses of a male defending his territory. Eve Carmichael wasn't his to defend. "She's visiting her sister on Tukamumu."

Eve flashed him a confused look, as though she couldn't understand his abrupt testiness. Heck, he was just as confused. Why the hell did he care that she didn't see him as her hero? He didn't. Besides, he was no hero, and frankly he was done rescuing women in distress.

Done, he repeated irritably. Just in case his thick skull hadn't got the message the first time.

"A doctor?" Teiki demanded, looking even more pleased—and impressed. "Kanaloa must have heard our prayers. Dr. Tahuru is having a hard time coping with all the injuries from last night's storm." He looked up into the sky and shrugged. "The next one's going to be even worse."

"Next one?" Eve said, looking up into the sky.

Chase could understand her confusion. It was crystal clear, as if last night's storm hadn't occurred.

"You can tell by looking at the sky?" she asked.

Teiki chuckled. "Well, the elders can," he said with a wink. "But my brother-in-law runs the local met station."

"Oh, I'm s-sorry," Eve stuttered, heat rising into her cheeks. "I didn't mean—"

"No worries, Doctor." Teiki laughed, gently patting her shoulder with a huge hand. "We take as much pride in our island's unspoilt beauty as we do in our hospital, school and met center." He shrugged. "If we want to compete with tourist destinations like Tahiti, Bora Bora and—" he winked at Chase, confusing Eve "—Tukamumu, then we have to be able to track storms and stay connected to the outside world. Which reminds me—" He gestured to the boat. "Why don't we take you to the resort so you can get cleaned up and rested? You must be starving. I'd open my home, but we had to take in family whose houses were damaged in the storm."

Chase wanted to refuse. Why, he had no idea. He *was*

starving. *And* he was overjoyed that they were on an inhabited island. That way he could contact his brother and get out of here sooner rather than later. That way he could make Eve someone else's responsibility.

That way he could salvage what was left of his freaking mind.

"That's a great idea," he said, shoving his hands in his pockets. His fingers touched something soft and flimsy and in a moment of confusion he nearly whipped it out, recalling at the last instant that he'd pocketed her underwear.

No. *Lingerie.*

The word conjured up an image of her wearing nothing but those pieces of silk and lace. Gulping, he pulled his hand out as though he'd been bitten and shoved his fingers through his hair, feeling—*what the hell?*—rattled.

"Why don't you…um…go ahead, Doc?" he stuttered, wondering when he'd turned into an awkward adolescent.

The thought panicked him and he suddenly couldn't get away fast enough. Besides, the break would keep him from doing something dumb. Like kissing her again.

Or worse.

She blinked at him as if he was abandoning her to a volcano-worshipping hostile tribe and he had to steel himself against making promises he couldn't keep. Promises he sure as hell didn't *want* to keep.

"What about you?"

"I need to salvage my cargo." He turned to Teiki. "Can you send the boat back for me?"

"I can do one better," the teacher announced, and gestured to the men waiting beside the boat. "Timéo and Bradley can take the doctor to the resort and return with a second boat. The rest of us will help with your cargo."

For some reason that she couldn't explain, Eve experienced a moment of panic at the thought of leaving Chase. But the sexy pirate who'd sucked the breath from her lungs just a half hour before had been replaced by a distant stranger, reminiscent of the man she'd met yesterday.

And so, because he seemed almost eager to be rid of her, Eve allowed Timéo to guide her to the boat. She watched as Chase held an intense discussion with Teiki, then disappeared into the trees without so much as a glance in her direction.

She wanted to pretend she didn't care, but when the big islander sent her an encouraging wave and headed up the beach after Chase, she felt lost. Which was just ridiculous. She wasn't lost. Just the opposite.

They'd just been rescued, for heaven's sake.

Besides, she was a big girl. She'd been taking care of herself—and everyone else—for a long time. There was absolutely no need to feel abandoned just because her sexy, grumpy pilot had left her with strangers.

Okay, he was essentially a stranger himself, and he was definitely not *hers*. But somehow he'd become…*more*. Which was somewhat alarming. As alarming as her childish feelings of abandonment.

Timéo must have sensed her distress, because he smiled reassuringly while Bradley pushed them away from the beach and jumped into the boat.

The engine puttered to life and they were soon heading out of the small cove and up the coast. The two men chatted quietly, leaving Eve feeling confused and disoriented about everything that had happened: the storm, the crash, their rescue…the—

Oh, no. Nope. Absolutely not. She was not going to think about the ki—*that.*

Besides, too much had happened in such a short space of time, leaving Eve reeling at the speed with which her life was changing…*she* was changing.

Worst of all, her life back home abruptly seemed like something she'd only read about.

Feeling a little freaked, she wrapped her arms around

herself and wondered if there was something on these islands that messed with people's minds, making them forget about their pasts. Making them think they'd finally arrived in Nirvana.

A light, balmy breeze brushed against her damp skin, sending an army of goose bumps swarming across her flesh. It reminded her that she'd had to dress in a hurry and that her pilot was walking around with her underwear in his pocket.

It also reminded her that the instant he'd realized they were being rescued he hadn't been able to wait to get rid of her. But she wouldn't think about that. Not now, she decided, gazing up at the island's jagged volcanic peaks that stretched into the sky and seemed to snatch clouds out of thin air.

Maybe later, when she'd recovered her mind.

After she'd found her sister, stopped her from making a huge mistake with some island bum and returned to her life.

Yep. Good plan.

She sighed. *Only* plan.

All too soon the boat was rounding a lushly vegetated headland. Eve noticed isolated bungalows hidden amid exotic jungle foliage that looked like something out of a honeymoon catalogue for the rich and famous.

Further up, the main resort grew out of the jungle, looking picturesque and strangely as if it had been part of the wild surroundings for centuries. The closer they got to the dock, the more people she could pick out—clearing storm debris, shoring up damaged buildings and carting away what looked like a ton of driftwood.

Seeing the destruction reminded her of Teiki's promise of another storm.

She turned to the islander steering the boat. "Is there really another storm on the way?" she asked as Bradley made for a long wooden dock jutting about fifty yards out into the bay.

He cut the engine, nodding at the thin line of clouds on the far horizon. "It's expected to reach us by midafternoon—maybe sooner."

Timéo leaped onto the jetty even before the boat gently bumped against the row of tires above the waterline and held out his hand to Eve. "I will accompany you to the resort," he said shyly. "Mr. Gallagher would like you to be comfortable."

Eve grabbed his hand and stepped onto the sturdy wooden planks, thinking that what "Mr. Gallagher" really wanted was to be rid of her.

Pushing aside that unwelcome thought, Eve thanked Bradley for his help and followed him along the wooden jetty. She was starving. She wanted a bath—and coffee—in the worst way possible and she didn't need a big strong man to get it for her.

She couldn't help noticing the curious glances she received as they made their way into the hotel, and wondered if she looked as bad as she imagined.

Timéo approached the front desk and a young woman looked up, her dark eyes widening when she caught sight of Eve.

Okay, so that certainly answered her question. The woman's expression didn't do much for her feminine pride, but there wasn't a lot she could do about it. She had no change of clothes, no money and—*dammit*, she thought, trying not to squirm—no underwear.

The receptionist sent her a smile of sympathy and nodded at whatever Timéo had said. He finally turned to Eve.

"Kimiki is my cousin." He smiled reassuringly. "She will take good care of you."

Eve reached out and touched his arm. "Thank you for your help."

"It was no trouble at all, Doctor," he replied with a flash of white teeth. "We are happy you are safe. *Ia ora na e Maeva*."

Then he turned and, with a wave, disappeared the way they had come, leaving Eve standing barefoot and a little dazed in the resort lobby.

It wasn't until she was finally alone in a spacious bathroom and caught sight of herself in the full-length mirror that she realized just how bad she looked.

Her mouth dropped open. *Yikes.* No wonder Chase had been so eager to get rid of her. She looked like something the sea had discarded along with all the other storm debris, while *he'd* just looked pirate hot.

She sighed. Her clothes were wrinkled and stained, her hair a damp, tangled mess, and she was covered in enough scrapes and bruises to make her look like—her mouth twisted at the irony—an air-crash survivor.

Quickly shedding her skirt and blouse, Eve stepped into the shower stall and turned on the water, groaning with appreciation when it hit her skin, hot and incredibly soothing.

Maybe there wasn't a bath, she told herself, but the shower—virtually open to the jungle and pouring hot, steaming water over her aching body—was the next best thing.

It was, she thought lifting her face, heaven. And for the first time since she'd opened her eyes in Port Laurent yesterday she felt like things were going to be okay.

All she needed was hot coffee and a huge breakfast, along with a couple hours' sleep, and she'd be able to face anything.

Chase let himself into the suite and moved toward the shutters, intending to open them and let in the bright morning light.

He needed a shower, clean clothes, food and sleep. Not necessarily in that order.

It wasn't until he had his hand on the shutter that he realized he wasn't alone. His head whipped around so fast he was momentarily dizzy. The instant his vision cleared his jaw dropped and he found himself gaping, his brain disconnected from the rest of his body.

The covers on the huge bed had been shoved aside. And there…in the middle…a *naked* Eve lay on her stomach, head turned away, her long, curvy form only partially covered by a snowy sheet.

Holy snickerdoodles!

Realizing he was staring—and possibly drooling— Chase snapped his mouth shut and shook his head. Then he heard something rattle and thought maybe his eyes had popped out and were rolling around on the floor somewhere.

He blinked a few times and when the vision remained, felt as though someone had sneaked up and punched him in the chest. His feet took him closer to the bed as his gaze swept up one long leg, uncovered right up to the sweet, familiar curve of a naked buttock.

He'd only had a quick glimpse of her on the beach, but now he let his greedy gaze take a more leisurely cruise over all that pale silky skin.

Honey-gold hair spilled across the pillow in a luxurious cloud and there, beneath her upraised arm, he could see the plump curve of one breast.

And suddenly, despite his exhaustion and pounding headache, his mouth watered. A dangerous interest stirred. An interest he didn't want to feel.

He instructed himself to leave, but the warm, smooth creamy skin that invited a man's touch was barely an arm's length away, tempting and even more dangerous to his health than a bed full of live rattlesnakes.

Shoving a hand through his hair, Chase grimly turned away. There was no way he could stay in the room and not think— He grunted softly, his mouth twisting dryly. Yeah, *those* kinds of thoughts. Thoughts better left unthought. Especially about a woman soon to be his brother's sister-in-law.

But it was already too late. He'd seen more than he should and less than he wanted. And now that was *all* he could think about.

Determined to do the right thing, Chase reached for the in-house phone and dialed the desk to request another suite. A minute later he carefully replaced the handset and scowled at the phone as if it had reared up and bitten him.

Great. Not even a storage closet available. He sighed. Unsurprising, really. It was peak tourist season, and whatever empty rooms they'd had were filled with guests from the bay units damaged in last night's storm. According to the receptionist, they'd been lucky to get this suite.

He eyed the huge comfortable bed—*and its occupant*—and sighed. *Yeah. Real lucky.*

But that was okay. He'd just pretend Eve was his ex and any spark of interest would be snuffed out. *Phfft.* Gone. Just like that.

So, yeah, they could share a bed. And he'd keep his hands—all his body parts—to himself.

No problem.

Absolutely no *problemo*.

CHAPTER SIX

FEET STUCK IN the bathroom doorway, Chase rubbed a towel over his dripping hair and glared at the naked woman sprawled across the bed. Completely oblivious to his misery.

The back of his skull tightened and he muttered a few choice curses.

So he had a problem. A number of problems, actually, the least of which was his wrecked plane. Nor was it that during his call to his brother, Jude, had made him promise not to reveal Amelia's little secret. Well, two secrets, actually—and neither of them could be termed "little" by any stretch of the imagination.

He'd had no problem agreeing because it wasn't his place to discuss family stuff that had nothing to do with him. And, frankly, his loyalty was to Jude and not to some woman he'd only just met.

He sighed. But that was for later. Right now his most pressing problem was asleep and taking up a good portion of the bed.

Okay. Bad idea, he realized, when his body decided to ignore the directive from his brain. Absolutely *not* going to think about long lengths of naked thigh. If he did it might be what finally made him cry like a girl, and he hadn't cried since the third grade, when Becca Thompson had bloodied his nose for using her waist-length pigtail as a paintbrush.

Sighing, he tossed the wet towel over his shoulder and moved into the room, heading for that tempting cloud of cool white. He was too damn tired and sore to care about *where* he crashed right now—no pun intended—as long as he crashed. Besides, he thought morosely as he probed the angry bruise covering his left shoulder, he deserved it after the past twenty-four hours.

Just minutes ago he'd caught sight of himself in the bathroom mirror and nearly laughed out loud at his reflection. It was no wonder people had given him a wide berth. He looked like he'd taken brawling to new heights—against an entire biker gang.

Yawning, he thrust a hand through his damp hair and contemplated his limited choices.

One: sleep on the floor. Two: shove the sexy doctor onto the floor and take the bed. Or three...

He snorted when he realized what he was doing. When the heck had he turned into such a wimp that he was running scared from a *woman*? A cool, I'm-all-professional one at that? Huffing out an irritated grunt, he decided the bed was big enough for them both. Besides, he was exhausted. Too exhausted to do anything his mind was conjuring up.

Maybe.

Tightening the knot on the towel around his waist, Chase took a determined step toward the bed and tried not to feel as though he was heading straight into a storm. And that this one might cost him more than his plane.

Persistent ringing penetrated Eve's sleep-fogged brain. Groaning softly, she groggily ran through her list of patients who could be in labor and came up empty.

She tried to reach for the phone but something warm and heavy had her pinned to the bed, and by the time she realized it was a body the ringing had stopped.

For a couple of seconds she freaked out, trying to remember who was in bed with her. Because drunken one-night stands had never been her thing and she hadn't had a relationship in a long time. A *very* long time. Not since the beginning of her specialist residency, in fact.

Frankly, she hadn't had the time or the energy.

There was, however, something familiar about the big body she was vacuum sealed against. Which was alarming enough, as she wasn't on intimate terms with any—

Memory returned between one heartbeat and the next and she recalled in vivid detail that not very long ago she'd awakened in a crashed plane in this exact same position. Only now she was—they were—*naked*.

Her eyes slammed open and she sucked in a shocked breath when she took in her position. She'd rolled right across the bed onto the side that had been unoccupied when she'd stretched out to consider her next step. The side that was currently occupied by—she squinted at the tanned chest and the eight-pack—her sexy, grumpy pilot.

She swallowed a whimper when she realized that that wasn't even the worst of it. She'd practically draped herself all over his delicious *naked* body as though she was a heat-seeking missile and he the center of the sun.

What the heck was he doing in her bed? And, more importantly, *what the heck was* she *doing snuggling up to a guy who island-hopped in the South Pacific to keep him in mai tais?*

Carefully, without moving a muscle, or even breathing, she took stock. Chase was on his back, his big body relaxed in sleep, dark silky hair falling in a tousled tumble across his forehead. And she… Well, she'd curled into his big body, one leg thrown over his, her head tucked under his chin. Her left hand was low on his belly, disturbingly close to… Well, never mind where. It had no business being there. As if she was staking her claim. As if her hand was accustomed to wandering into dangerous territory.

It wasn't. *She* wasn't. She had no interest in Chase Gallagher, or his big…*gulp*…ego, despite the fact that her body appeared to want to be close to his. His body appeared to want that too, as a muscled arm was wrapped around her and his big calloused hand was cupped possessively over one butt cheek.

And *darn* if her belly didn't give a quiver of interest and then promptly melt. She squeezed her eyes closed. No melting. Melting was bad.

Carefully expelling her breath, Eve began to ease away, but at the first movement his muscles tightened, rippling like a large hungry cat whose coveted meal was about to escape.

She stilled and waited a couple of seconds. When his breathing remained slow and steady she carefully lifted her head…to find his sleepy gaze locked on her.

Her heart gave one hard kick against her ribs before taking off like a frightened rabbit, sending blood pinging through her veins.

Making her dizzy. Snatching her breath.

Deciding that a good offence was the best defense, Eve accused, "You're in my bed."

A dark eyebrow arched as he took in her position, on his side of the bed…with her hand still close to ground zero. Ground zero that was in the process of waking up too.

Her eyes bugged. She gave an alarmed little squeak and tried to jerk away, but his grip tightened. And before she could demand to know what the heck he was doing or apologize for her body's behavior—*whatever!*—he'd flipped her over onto her back and was looming over her as if he intended making a meal of her.

The hard thigh between hers pinned her to the bed, bringing his ground zero terrifyingly close to hers.

Shocked by the ease with which he'd accomplished the move, Eve gaped up into his hard, handsome face. For a long moment his gray gaze was hot and fierce, then his attention dropped to her mouth, where it lingered a moment before traveling south to where her breasts, naked and tingling, were squashed up against all his sculpted magnificence.

His lips curled and, helplessly, Eve looked too. She nearly combusted on the spot.

After a breathless pause, his eyes burned a path from her breasts, up her throat and back to her mouth, setting fire to every nerve ending along the way. And when he dipped his head to trace a scorching path across her cheek to the corner of her mouth, she could do nothing more than suck in a sharp breath and wait for his next move.

His low chuckle had her every hair follicle tingling with excitement. She wanted to smack him for finding this amusing. It wasn't. She didn't want to feel this out of control, this desperate—not with him.

His smiling mouth skimmed hers, leaving her lips tingling with anticipation and frustration as he moved on, nipping at her chin, dipping to scrape his teeth along the tendon in her neck, before heading for the curve joining her neck and shoulder.

Expecting the same tantalizing, barely there torture, Eve felt her entire body jolt when his mouth opened and sucked her flesh into his hot mouth. And to her absolute horror a whimper escaped from her throat. Even worse, her nipples tightened into diamond-hard buds that he wouldn't be able to help but notice. Her belly flooded with a languid liquid heat that made her shudder and squeeze her thighs around his.

He must have liked that, because he groaned and pressed his thigh tighter, higher against her core.

Another shudder and a rush of liquid heat. She gasped. "Chase..." Oh, God. Was that *her* sounding so husky and... and needy? She wasn't. Or she wasn't normally. But something about Chase Gallagher brought out the worst in her. Made her want things she hadn't thought about in a long time. Made her yearn for the touch of another human being.

Okay—fine. A man. He made her yearn for the touch of

a man. But not him. Never him. He was too forceful, too demanding. Like now, as he dropped his head to nip at her breasts, demanding a response. And, *God*, her body was all too eager to give it to him, arching up as a low moan tore loose from somewhere deep in her belly.

He lifted his head. Tension crackled in the air between them as the hell-fire heat of his gaze burned into hers.

Holy cow. No one had ever looked at her with such naked *lust* before. It was wildly exciting and totally unnerving. So unnerving that when he murmured, "Do you want me to stop?" Eve opened her mouth and babbled, "No. *Yes!* I don't know..." before she could stop herself.

His chuckle was a dark, thrilling sound in the dim room, sending anticipation streaking across her skin and a bone-deep need vibrating in her core—along with a rush of mortification.

Way to sound sophisticated, Evelyn.

His next words, "Why don't I help you make up your mind?" were whispered against her skin, giving her a full-body flush.

She bit her lip to prevent an, *Oh, yes, please!* from escaping, because she had a feeling it wouldn't take much on his part to get her to agree. First because her body was already in full agreement, and second...second she was an inch away from climaxing. All from the touch of his mouth and the sound of his voice.

Well, that's just embarrassing. As was the impatient way her body moved against his. If she hadn't been half out of her mind with the way sensations zipped through her she might have been mortified that she was begging.

He lifted his head and their gazes held for a long, breathless beat. His hands smoothed circles of heat on her hip, then her thigh, moved up to her waist...and finally her ribs. His thumb flicked out to tease the bottom curve of her breast, drawing it into a tight, painful mound of need and entreaty.

Eve sucked in a breath, only just managing to stop a whimper from emerging—because if he'd meant his caresses to soothe he'd totally miscalculated. *Big-time.* All they had done was electrify her skin until even the most delicate touch made her want to scream.

Then finally...*oh, God, finally*...he leaned forward and opened his mouth over hers in a kiss as hot as it was hungry. And when she murmured into his mouth he deepened the kiss, his tongue sliding in to stroke hers.

Teasing was clearly over. *Thank God.*

She'd thought their kiss earlier today had been pretty darn hot, but it was nothing compared to this...this invasion of her senses. There was nothing playful about the way he just moved in and sucked the breath from her lungs, along with the rapidly fading notion that she should resist.

That she *could* resist.

You should at least try.

He was everything she didn't want in a man. He was too big, too bold...too *everything.* Including too good at making her forget what it was she was supposed to be doing.

Which was... *Oh, yeah.* She was supposed to be resisting, pushing him away. Escaping while she could still think.

Obeying the directive from her brain, her arms came up. But instead of pushing, they pulled him in, sliding their palms flat up his wide back to his shoulders. From there they headed up his strong neck and—*look at that!*—totally without her consent tunneled into his thick silky hair.

It was Chase's turn to shudder as her nails scraped against his scalp, his body jerking against hers. The realization that she had as much power over him as he had over her was a little overwhelming. And wildly exciting. Especially when she tried it again and he growled—a low, thrilling sound that had her going damp in secret places.

Her eyes fluttered closed and she let herself drift in the moment, enjoying the way his mouth felt plundering hers, his taste, the way each kiss fed the next and then another, until she was moaning and clinging to him—moving urgently against him in desperation.

She felt overwhelmed, soaking up his heat, his taste. His hard, hot thigh was sliding between hers and setting aflame nerve endings she'd hadn't realized existed.

He finally abandoned her mouth to slide his lips down her throat and lick the hollow at its base before moving on. Her breasts tingled in anticipation, the nipples hardening into tight little buds of eagerness.

But, *dammit*, instead of taking them in his mouth he merely skimmed the inside curve of her cleavage before heading south once more, smiling at her moan of frustration.

His tongue painted her skin with heated swipes, dipping into her shallow belly button and soothing the small pain he'd created by gently nipping at her hip with his teeth.

Goose bumps erupted and the muscles deep in her belly clenched against the urge to explode.

"Chase..." she moaned, unsure of what she'd been about to say because he'd robbed her of the ability to think, to do anything but feel. And, boy, she was feeling a whole heck of a lot—including excitement and heat. And something along the lines of—*ohmigod!* He nudged her legs apart and his mouth headed...right into dangerous territory.

Just when she thought she might die if he didn't put his mouth on her the phone began ringing again, the sound an unwelcome jangle in the heated silence.

Eve jolted like she'd been shot. Chase froze, his grip on her tightening. Their eyes met down the length of her body, and when she saw his mouth barely an inch from... *yikes!*...it abruptly dawned on her what he'd been about to do. What she been on the verge of *letting* him do.

With a squeak of embarrassment Eve lurched upwards, slamming her legs together.

Eyes blazing molten heat, Chase stretched out a long

arm to snatch up the phone, the movement vibrating with barely leashed violence.

"Yeah?" he growled, and Eve felt a moment's empathy for whoever was at the other end. But then his eyes sharpened and cleared. "The doctor? She's an..." His eyebrows rose in query. "Obstetrician?" When she silently nodded, he said, "A doctor's a doctor, right? All right, I'll tell her."

He listened for another few moments before sitting up and replacing the receiver with studied casualness. With his back to her, he shoved both hands through his hair and expelled his breath on a ragged laugh, clearly wondering what the heck they'd both been thinking.

They hadn't been thinking, Eve admitted, that was the problem. He'd put his mouth on her and she'd lost brain cells. Brain cells she could scarcely afford to lose—especially to a huge mistake. And this...them...would be a mistake. At least it would be for her.

She wasn't a one-night stand kind of woman, and he... Well, for all she knew he most likely wasn't anything else.

Furthermore, she didn't know all that much about him. Other than that he was a sexy, grumpy pilot, mourning the loss of his seaplane like it was his best friend, and that he kissed like he really knew his way around a woman's body. Oh, and he looked good in a pair of cargoes—*really* good—which was difficult for *anyone* to pull off.

Realizing she was lying there naked and exposed, Eve snatched the sheet and yanked it up to her chin, waging an internal battle about whether she was relieved or disappointed they'd been interrupted.

Then he glanced over his shoulder at her. Definitely relieved. Especially as the eyes that had been smoky with heat just a few moments ago were now cool and unreadable. As though his mouth *hadn't* been an inch from her...

Her belly clenched and embarrassment heated her cheeks, because he clearly hadn't been as affected by what had almost happened. Sucking in a shaky breath, she tried to look relaxed—as though it had been nothing. As though she did this all time when in fact it rarely happened. Obviously he was a lot more experienced at this sort of thing than she was.

On the other hand, she wasn't blind. And when he rose and headed for the bathroom she got an eyeful of the erection he was sporting. It drew a muffled gasp and a hot flash, because…*wow*…the man had heft—and girth.

She gave a silent snort. Okay, so maybe he hadn't been as unaffected as she'd thought. Because that erection certainly wasn't *"nothing."*

And neither was the wild leap of her pulse at the sight of him in all his glorious nakedness.

But that could just be relief, she hastily assured herself. Relief that she'd escaped before she'd made the biggest mistake of her life with a man she barely knew.

He was opinionated, rude and irascible, and he liked having fun at her expense. She was obviously suffering from low blood sugar and an overload of potent pheromones if she was lusting after someone who was happy flying around the South Pacific just because it kept him in fancy cocktails.

But, boy, his body was hard—brawny and aggressive in a way that made a woman stick out her chest and reach for her lipgloss. It vibrated with barely leashed violence—testament to the fact that his blood was probably 90 percent testosterone.

She'd learned early on that alpha males couldn't be trusted. And it was as clear as the tanned skin on his tight buns that he was alpha from the top of his sleep-mussed dark hair to his big, brawny feet.

Face it, she told herself firmly, *there's nothing to get all worked up about.*

He was just a guy. An annoying one at that.

Not attractive at all.

Eve snorted and rolled her eyes.

Who the heck was she kidding? He was magnificent. All hard planes and rippling muscles. Every inch of him gorgeous and tempting...begging to be touched...licked.

But not by her, she reminded herself firmly.

Nope. He was definitely not the man for her.

He turned suddenly, catching her in the act of ogling his sexy body. His chuckle was a low rumble in the quiet room. He was obviously amused to be the object of her lustful glances.

Heat and mortification flooded her. *Darn*. What the heck *was* it about this man that made her act like a silly blushing adolescent? It had to stop. Right now.

Tucking the sheet beneath her armpits, she licked her lips and inched her way to the opposite edge of the bed.

Time to start acting like an adult, Evelyn.

"Who was on the...uh...phone?"

Chase casually snagged a towel off the bed, and when he'd wrapped it around his narrow waist and tucked in the ends she sighed with relief. Now maybe she could think.

"Front desk. One of the guests is suffering from stomach pains and her husband is asking for a doctor."

"Isn't there a clinic on the island?"

"There is. But apparently she's almost doubled over in pain, and since you're closer he wondered if you'd have a look at her." He glanced toward the window. "Her husband doesn't want to travel into town if it's something minor. Not with the next storm practically on our doorstep."

"Do they know I'm a gynecologist?"

"They do now. But you studied medicine before you specialized, right? A stomach ache should be child's play."

Hardly child's play if it was a symptom of something serious...

Nibbling on her lip, Eve felt her mind race as she sorted through the reasons anyone might have severe stomach pain. "Does she have abdominal bloating or swelling? Leg pain? Pelvic pain before her menstrual cycle? Painful intercourse? Breast tenderness? Nausea…vomiting?"

There was a short silence, and when she looked up it was to see Chase staring at her like she was asking if he had a foot fungus.

Her brow wrinkled. "What?"

He shook his head, looking a little panicked. As if he'd been trapped with a crazy person and was casting around for an escape.

He exhaled noisily. "You don't really expect me to answer that, do you?" He huffed out a disbelieving laugh. "Firstly, what guy asks any woman about painful sex? And menstrual cycles…?" He looked like he'd swallowed something bad. "You're *kidding*, right?"

Eve sighed. She might have been crazy to start this wild goose chase, but when it came to medicine she was clearheaded and focused, often to the point of obsession. She sometimes forgot nonmedical guys got a little weird when it came to "women's problems."

"I just thought—"

"Well, you thought wrong," he interrupted hastily, looking like he was thinking about bolting, and she paused to enjoy the mental picture of him streaking through the hotel in just his towel. "Believe me when I say those are things I never discuss. *Ever.*" He shuddered. When she just stared at him, he demanded, "Well?"

"Well, what?"

"Go and do…whatever it is women doctors do. And please ask someone else those questions."

Eve hid a smile and finally looked down at herself. "I can hardly go out wearing a sheet," she pointed out. "My clothes are wrecked and—" She blushed. "And you…um… stole my underwear."

Relieved not to be talking about periods and painful intercourse with the woman he'd almost had sex with, Chase tilted his head and studied her. Wrapped in a sheet and looking all flushed and flustered, like she'd just been ravished, she was one big temptation he didn't need.

Another minute and he would have been buried deep inside her body—which clearly meant he should be grateful they'd been interrupted. Especially as he hadn't given a thought to protection.

That thought was enough to scare him rigid.

Okay, he amended, looking down at the tented towel. Maybe not rigid... But he had been an eager participant, and didn't know whether to thank the concierge or beat the hell out of him for interrupting what would most certainly have been a spectacular ravishing.

Besides, he reminded himself, she wasn't his type and he clearly wasn't hers.

Good. Great. They were both not each other's type.

Message received.

"I don't know," he said, scratching his jaw. "I think it suits you."

Eve rolled her eyes, obviously relieved to change the subject. "Please. I look like I'm dressed for a sorority toga party."

Chase's mouth curved at the vision that popped into his head. "Yeah," he said, recalling the toga parties he'd attended in his sophomore year that had all but descended into debauchery. "Looks great."

She cast a disbelieving look at herself. "Great?"

Suddenly the idea of anyone seeing Eve walking out of the suite looking like an ancient Roman delicacy made his brow furrow in displeasure. She was right, he decided. She needed clothes. Preferably a sack that covered her from head to toe.

Yeah, and he was an idiot.

"You didn't happen to...um—" She broke off, looking away, clearly embarrassed.

Intrigued, Chase studied her closely and decided he

liked seeing her flustered. She was softer and a lot less the sophisticated professional. Very appealing. And also very bad. Especially bad were the ideas it gave him.

She was still staring at him. He had no idea what she'd been saying, so he went with, "What?"

She grimaced. "Find my bags? In the wreckage, I mean?"

He opened his mouth to admit that he hadn't even given it a thought but, "I thought you didn't have a change of clothes with you?" emerged instead.

"I don't. I need my wallet to…um…pay for a few things from the hotel boutique."

He shrugged. "Don't worry about it. The company will pay for anything you need. Just charge it to the room."

"I'd rather pay for it myself," Ms. Independence countered primly. "Besides, I need my passport and airline tickets." She lifted her head, glowing amber eyes beseeching now. "Please tell me you found my bags. I…I need my phone. I need to get home."

"I thought you needed to stop your sister from making a huge mistake by marrying some loser she's only just met?" he said a little sarcastically.

"Well, yes…" she said, looking confused by his sarcasm. "But after that I intend going back to London. I'm supposed to be at a medical conference. I'm also waiting for a DC medical center to let me know about a position I applied for."

Chase rubbed his hands over his face and shook his head. "Nope," he said with a head shake. "We didn't find anything."

Eve sucked in an audible breath, looking like she was on the verge of a full-blown panic attack, so he hitched one shoulder helplessly.

"We crashed in a really dense part of the island," he explained. "It could take days…weeks…to search the area and you'd still probably never find anything. It's so humid out here that the jungle reclaims everything in a matter of days.

"So…" She sucked in another deep breath, struggling to stay calm. "You're telling me I'm stuck here in…the middle of the South Pacific…indefinitely? Without a passport or a way to get home?"

He mentally cursed his lack of foresight. "That about covers it. You can use my computer on Tukamumu to contact the embassy. But I need to warn you that life…official life, that is…moves at a different pace out here."

She paled and looked a little sick, and again he cursed himself—because the loss of her passport meant she was going to be around awhile. Which abruptly seemed like the worst thing that could happen.

For him at least.

He studied the picture she made, sitting there all soft and sexy, nibbling on that wide, plump bottom lip, and recalled something Jude had said about Amelia's childhood.

It had been bad. Bad enough that from an early age Eve had taken on the role of caregiver and protector—all the while working herself through high school and then med school.

Yet here she was; looking young and fresh and as untouched as a schoolgirl. No sign of that backbone of steel.

He thrust an unsteady hand through his hair. You had to admire the hell out of someone with that much grit. But accompanying his admiration was the realization that he was in trouble.

Biiiiig trouble.

Sexy, silky woman trouble. From her tawny hair and golden-syrup eyes to her small, elegant feet.

Oh, yeah. He was screwed.

CHAPTER SEVEN

EVE FOLLOWED A uniformed employee across the patio, shocked to see that while she'd been sleeping—and crawling all over a certain sexy pilot—an ominous bank of clouds had swept across the sea toward them, dispelling this morning's image of a forgotten Eden.

Trouble, it seemed, was a lot closer than the horizon.

Wind gusted in from the bay, setting the palms and banana trees rustling an urgent warning of the oncoming storm. It had turned the sea an eerie gunmetal gray, far removed from the clear, calm turquoise of this morning.

Despite the fact that it wasn't cold, Eve shivered. The sight of those towering black clouds and flashes of lightning brought back memories of the crash and...well, stuff she'd rather not think about.

Like being stranded without money or her passport.

Much better to think about— *Oh, boy.* A flush moved through her until she thought she was probably glowing like a luminescent glowstick in the early gloom.

Okay, maybe not. Maybe she should think instead of the reason she was on this very vulnerable piece of volcanic rock, stuck in the middle of the Pacific instead of in London.

Amelia.

Who'd most likely expected her yesterday and was probably thinking the worst right about now. That Eve was shark bait.

And Eve was thinking about a tanned eight-pack, long, muscular legs and tight buns, instead of a way to reach her sister.

She was certain that she just needed to hear Amelia's voice and all those unwelcome emotions would disappear. Clearly she wasn't the only twin susceptible to tropical islands. Maybe she just needed a healthy dose of reality. Like…like those clouds, for one. Another thought hit her and she groaned. Or maybe it was something more basic. Something along the lines of the potent cocktail of testosterone and pheromones that surrounded Chase Gallagher like a toxic cloud of doom and made her misbehave.

Staying away from him would be the smart thing to do. And Eve had always done the smart thing.

Always.

Feeling very unprofessional, in a brightly colored muu-muu—the island version of a sarong—silk panties and a pair of flip flops, Eve waited while the porter knocked on a suite door.

A man in his mid-thirties answered and did a double-take when he saw her. Had he expected someone older? More professional-looking? Someone not covered in bruises?

"Hi," he said, looking a little frazzled. "I'm…uh…Mark. Are you…?"

"Hello, Mark. My name is Dr. Eve Carmichael. How can I help you?"

"I…I don't know what's wrong with my…uh…wife, Raina," he explained hurriedly. "She's in a lot of pain. We thought that by this morning it would be okay, but it's worse. *She's* worse." A muffled groan came from behind him and he cast a haunted look over his shoulder. "Oh, God, I don't know what to—"

"Why don't you let me come in?" Eve interrupted gently.

He hesitated another moment, his gaze taking in her casual attire and her bruises, before taking a step back. "You're really a doctor?" When Eve just looked at him he shoved a hand through his rumpled hair. "I honestly don't know what I was expecting. The concierge was using words like *rongoa* and *tohunga*, and I kind of assumed…"

He gave an embarrassed laugh and closed the door behind her. Eve frowned and studied him with assessing eyes, wondering if he'd been drinking or taking recreational drugs.

"Rongoa? Tohunga?" Eve shook her head in confusion at the unfamiliar words. "I'm sorry, I don't know what that means."

He led the way through the suite. "Apparently it's a kind of healer. A *tohunga* is a specialist, or something."

He hovered in the bedroom doorway and Eve had to brush past him.

"We're smack-dab in the middle of the South Pacific," he said on a loud whoosh of air. "Thousands of miles from the nearest city. I half expected a medicine man to arrive at our door."

"Oh, I don't think they have those anymore," Eve said drily.

The young woman curled on the bed was pale, her lovely features twisted in pain and slick with perspiration.

"Hi," Eve said, gently taking Raina's wrist and unerringly finding her pulse. "I'm a doctor. An OB-GYN specialist, actually."

"Really?" Mark said, skepticism written all over his smooth handsome face. "You're a little young, aren't you? And you look…" He gestured to her battered face and the bruises covering the rest of her.

"We were forced to land in the storm," she murmured absently. "It was a little rough."

He snorted. "I'd say more than 'a little rough.' Maybe you should sue the airline?"

Eve looked up to see if he was serious. He was. "The airline and the pilot weren't at fault," she said mildly, even though the pilot *was* responsible for at least two of her bruises. The hickey on her neck and the first bump on her head. "Lightning struck the engine."

Without waiting for him to reply, she turned back to her patient.

"Are you pregnant?"

"Pregnant?" Mark burst out, horrified.

A flash of something indefinable crossed the young woman's face and she hurriedly shook her head, lowering her eyes. Eve caught the quick flash of tears and sent Mark a speculative look across her shoulder.

He looked appalled. And green.

"You never said anything about being pregnant, Raina," he accused angrily. "If you had I never would have—" He stopped abruptly when he realized both Eve and Raina were gaping at him, stunned by his outburst.

Tears sparkled in Raina's eyes. "I'm not—I promise. It's something else. It's got to be."

Without taking her eyes off Mark, Eve asked quietly, "Would you feel better if Mark left the room while I examine you?"

The young woman bit her lip and nodded, carefully avoiding looking at her husband. After a short, tension-filled moment Mark sighed and left, closing the door behind him. Once he'd left Eve gently probed the young woman's abdomen, noting her soft cry of pain.

"Now that your husband has gone," Eve said quietly as she continued her examination, "I'm going to ask you why you don't want him to know you're pregnant."

Raina sucked in a sharp breath and shook her head. "I'm not," she rasped, looking distressed. "I *can't* be."

"Raina—"

"Look, Mark isn't my husband," she confessed in a low voice, her gaze sliding away from Eve's. "He's my b-boss."

She gave a muffled sob. "My *m-married* boss. I can't... He'll f-fire me. Besides, I c-couldn't be. It's not possible. I thought...I thought it might be my appendix?"

Eve was continuing with her examination. "Tell me why it's not possible?" she asked gently.

Raina went on to explain that she'd been spotting for a few days, and experiencing the lower abdominal and back pain which she assured Eve was normal for the first couple of days of her cycle.

On further probing Eve discovered that the pain had started in her right side and moved to the left, until her pelvic area was very painful, making it hard for her to walk upright, which was why she'd thought it was her appendix. She was nauseous, exhausted and kept needing the bathroom.

Eve then posed the same questions to her that she'd asked Chase, and by the time she was finished with her examination she was convinced it wasn't dysmenorrhea, appendicitis, kidney stones or even ovarian cysts.

If she was right, the woman would likely need surgery. Very soon. Especially if the bleeding worsened and she went into shock.

Eve smoothed Raina's hair off her clammy forehead. "I don't want you to worry," she said firmly. "We're going to take good care of you."

She rose and left the room. This was a procedure that needed a team of physicians, preferably in a sterile environment. Raina needed a hospital.

She found a pale Mark waiting nervously in the small lounge, slugging back three fingers of whiskey while he paced. Ignoring his signs of extreme agitation, she explained that further tests were needed and that Raina needed to go to the hospital immediately.

"She's pregnant, isn't she?" he demanded a little wildly. "Dammit, I *knew* it. I should have—"

"I need to run a few tests to confirm my diagnosis," Eve

interrupted coolly. "And I can only do that at a hospital. It's imperative that we go immediately."

He shoved his hand in his hair, looking really rattled beneath the anger. "But... But..."

"Look," she said firmly, trying not to judge his attitude, which she suspected was more about not getting caught by his wife than ensuring his mistress received proper medical attention. "If we don't get Raina to the nearest hospital— and this island has one," she informed him briskly, "she could die." She waited for the news to sink in before adding, "I'm sure you don't want that to happen to your *wife*."

He turned red. "She's not my...um..." His breath escaped in a loud whoosh when Eve's eyebrow rose up her forehead. "No," he said, avoiding her level gaze. "I don't want that to happen."

"Good. Then I suggest you phone the concierge and request a car. We don't have a moment to lose."

The wind had picked up, sending trees and palms bending at impossible angles. Eve glanced worriedly at the black clouds barreling toward them and sucked in a nervous breath when a powerful gust hit the car broadside.

She'd never seen anything as angry and scary as those towering, boiling columns, and couldn't help wondering what was heading their way.

Nothing good—that was for certain.

Was the shiver of premonition sliding down her spine due to the storm—or something else?

Fortunately the driver didn't waste time, racing along the deserted roads toward town. Eve didn't know if he was aware of their urgency or just wanted to get home before the storm broke.

She wouldn't blame him if it was the latter. After yesterday's experience she wanted to be somewhere safe too. Like in London. Or Washington. Even if they were knee-deep in snow.

The hotel must have called ahead. A couple of orderlies waited at Emergency, rushing out with a wheelchair. Eve introduced herself and was surprised when the men traded significant glances.

"Is something wrong?" she asked as she and Mark helped Raina out of the car.

"Oh, no," the older man said quickly. "We heard how you and Mr. Chase crashed in last night's storm."

"Oh?"

The younger of the two blushed and Eve wondered what else they'd heard, and if it had anything to do with her introduction to the islanders. When Eve had been caught swimming naked by a boatful of gaping men.

"Yeah," he said with a wide smile. "Teiki said that Lono and Kanaloa must have brought you here for a purpose."

"Lono? Kanaloa?" she asked, keeping a hard hold on Mark as she followed them into the clinic. He was strung tighter than chicken wire. The muscled arm in her grip vibrated with a tension that she suspected was a desire to bolt at the first opportunity.

"Polynesian deities," a smooth voice cut in, and Eve turned as a middle-aged woman approached.

She was dressed in a lab coat, with a stethoscope around her neck, and her brisk no-nonsense attitude identified her as a doctor. She couldn't be anything else. Not with that quietly efficient yet unmistakably authoritative aura.

Eve stepped forward and offered her hand. "You must be Dr. Tahuru."

The older woman smiled and clasped Eve's in a firm handshake. "And you're the specialist the storm brought to our island."

Eve felt herself flush under the woman's amused scrutiny. She let out a breathless laugh. "You heard about the crash?" *And possibly about how they'd been found.*

Dr. Tahuru grinned, her sharp eyes assessing first Eve

and then Raina. "We're a small community. News travels fast."

She instructed an orderly to take the patient and her husband to a nearby exam room before turning to Eve.

"Have you examined her, Dr. Carmichael?"

"I did, yes," she admitted. "At the…the husband's request."

"And?"

"I suspect an ectopic pregnancy, but you'll need to run a few tests."

Dr. Tahuru sucked in a sharp breath and cast a worried look out the ER door. "I'm a general practitioner," she explained. "And this is a very small facility. Any serious cases are usually sent to Rangiroa or Raitea."

"I'm afraid she doesn't have time for that," Eve said quietly. "If I'm right, she's going to need surgery tonight."

Dr. Tahuru narrowed her eyes and quietly studied Eve, obviously weighing her up. Eve knew what she saw. Dressed in a sarong and flip-flops, and without make-up, she looked like a teenager.

She held her breath. The last thing she wanted was to offend the woman, or the island's customs, and appear as though she wanted to take over, so she waited, holding the doctor's gaze with quiet intensity.

Working in a large city hospital had the benefit of letting her encounter a host of unusual cases, but she'd never done laparoscopies or performed a laparotomy in anything but a well-equipped OR. Or without an attending anesthetist.

A laparoscopy was less invasive, but the question here was, did the tiny facility have the equipment?

After a couple of beats Dr. Tahuru gave a decisive nod. "Very well, Dr. Carmichael, let's find you some scrubs."

Ninety minutes later Eve and Jasmine Tahuru scrubbed up as they discussed the procedure. The HCG test and sonogram had come back positive. Raina Ellis was pregnant, and the fetus was growing in the right fallopian tube.

Given her symptoms, Eve suspected the young woman didn't have time for any more tests. At the last check her BP had dropped and she'd complained of shoulder pain, which meant the fallopian tube had ruptured and was leaking blood into her abdomen. If she was lucky it wouldn't be a serious tear and Eve wouldn't have to remove the entire fallopian.

Entering the tiny OR through the scrub room door, Eve glanced around and felt a moment's apprehension that was tinged with excitement. She usually felt both just before surgery, but this time her apprehension resulted from the knowledge that the room only contained the basics.

Which meant they'd have to operate.

Her excitement, she admitted silently, was caused by the notion that she'd have to rely on her skills without the aid of high-tech equipment.

Raina was already on the table, anxiously waiting. She gave a low sob when she saw Eve in a surgical gown, her eyes filling with tears as the seriousness of her situation finally registered. Her grip was fierce when Eve took her hand.

"Hey," Eve said with a reassuring smile. "You're going to be fine, I promise. Dr. Tahuru has been running this hospital for almost as long as you've been alive. She's probably seen just about everything. You're in good hands, I promise."

"I still can't believe I'm pregnant. How did I not know?"

Eve continued prepping her while Jasmine fitted electrode discs to Raina's upper chest. "Many women have periods during pregnancy," she said gently. "It's not uncommon." She waited a couple of beats while the young woman processed that, before saying quietly, "But maybe you should think about making a few changes when you get home. You owe it to yourself."

A look of unhappiness crossed Raina's face and she bit her lip before saying in a low, fierce voice, "You're right. I do." She blinked away her tears. "I finally realized he's just been stringing me along. I'd heard rumors, but I thought… He made me feel so…special." She sniffed miserably as she faced the truth. "He really has no intention of leaving his wife, does he?"

"I can't say," Eve responded reluctantly. Frankly, judging by Mark's reaction to her diagnosis, he probably wouldn't. "But you deserve a man willing to commit fully."

Raina inhaled shakily. "You'll be here, though. Won't you?"

Eve smiled and applied a saturation probe to her finger, listening as the quiet beeping filled the room. "I'm not going anywhere," she assured her, lifting her head to catch the other doctor's level look. "Let's finish getting you prepped. When you wake up you can start making those plans."

Eve waited until Raina Ellis was under before lifting her scalpel. "We'll have to be quick," she told Dr. Tahuru. "Even with a light anesthetic we can't keep her under too long without an anesthetist."

"Florine will watch her vitals." She paused while Eve nodded at the veteran nurse. "Ready when you are, Doctor."

Eve sucked in a deep breath, lifted her mask into place and said a quick prayer. She was aiming for a quick in-and-out procedure, and as she made the first transverse incision along the bikini line she said, "The main concern here is to stop any hemorrhaging and remove all traces of trophoblastic cells." She paused as Dr. Tahuru mopped the welling blood. "We don't want them reattaching and growing again."

She gently exposed the tube and waited while Dr. Tahuru applied clamps to either side of the gestational sac.

Jasmine peered closer. "What's that? About four, five weeks?"

"Hmm…" Eve murmured, carefully examining the ovary and uterus for signs of trauma. She gave a quick sigh of relief. They were intact. She gently exposed the sac to evaluate the area of attachment. "Looks about right. Fortunately the rupture is close to the attachment site. We should be able to dislodge it with minimal damage."

Thirty minutes later, and after a hair-raising incident during which they'd thought they wouldn't be able to stop the bleeding without removing the entire fallopian tube, Eve released the suture ligature she'd applied a few minutes earlier and held her breath.

When no new blood appeared she exhaled loudly, and waited while Jasmine flushed the tube. She then carefully placed a few microsutures along the rupture to keep the edges together and began closing her up.

"What about scarring along the tube?" Jasmine asked, injecting antibiotics into a bag of Ringer's lactate solution and closing off the port dispensing the anesthetic. "Won't that narrow it?"

"That is a concern," Eve murmured, working a suture with quick, efficient hands. "She'll have to visit her gynecologist when she gets home. A laparoscopy will determine if there is any scarring that could cause future egg implantation. If that happens they will most likely remove the tube completely. I'm hoping that won't be necessary."

Eve completed the final suture and checked Raina's vitals. It had been forty minutes.

"Neatly done, Doctor," Jasmine said. "Why don't you tell the 'husband' while I finish up here?"

Her dark eyes gleamed over the top of her mask when Eve groaned.

"I think it'll be better coming from you."

Mark had made enough noise earlier about "backwoods hospitals and incompetent medical staff" that she understood Jasmine's sentiments.

Eve shook her head. "It'd be better coming from a man, you mean," she said drily. "He's obviously one of *those*."

"Those?"

"You know—those men who think woman are good for only one thing."

"We get that all the time," the older woman agreed. "Some men still haven't entered the twenty-first century."

Especially as there were still women willing to let them continue with their antiquated beliefs. Her mother had always looked for men who would take care of her.

Yeah. And look how *that* had turned out. Knocked up and abandoned—not once, but twice.

Sighing, Eve stepped away from the table and stripped off the double-layered latex gloves. She dropped them into the disposal bin on her way to the door. She was accustomed to dealing with rude next of kin. She didn't like it, but she understood that some people reacted to fear and stress by being obnoxious.

And Mark had been as obnoxious as they came. He was certainly handsome, but Eve didn't understand the appeal. At least not beyond the first five minutes.

She found him pacing the small private waiting room. He spotted her immediately and headed over, looking like he was working on an internal storm to rival the one brewing outside.

Eve had opened her mouth to tell him he was heading for a stroke and should learn to relax when the irony hit her. She sucked in a shocked breath instead. Here she was, the queen of stress, about to advise someone to relax. When the heck had *that* happened? She lifted her hand to the bump on her forehead and frowned. Maybe she really did have brain damage.

"I've been here three hours and no one will tell me what the hell is going on!" Mark snapped, scowling at her as though he was accustomed to intimidating everyone he perceived as inferior. "What kind of hospital is this, anyway? It doesn't have a cafeteria or even a vending machine, for God's sake. And no one speaks any English."

Eve ignored his outburst. She could understand his agitation, if not his prejudice. And plenty of people on the island spoke English if you didn't treat them with arrogant superiority.

"The procedure went well," she said calmly, determined to be civil. Even if it cost her. And it did cost her—especially when his eyes sharpened at her words.

"She's no longer pregnant?"

Eve ground her teeth together. No matter how much she might want to, punching him in the mouth wasn't the answer. Mark wasn't one of her mother's boyfriends, and this wasn't *her* drama. Even if it brought back memories from her childhood. Bad memories of constant fighting and unwelcome attention from her mother's man du jour, especially after she and Amelia reached puberty.

"No," she said quietly. "She's no longer pregnant."

He stared at her for a couple of beats, as though struggling to absorb the news. Then naked relief filled his eyes and he choked out a rusty laugh. "Oh, thank God!" he burst out, shoving shaking fingers through his already rumpled hair. He caught Eve's expression and froze. "I mean...I don't... You can't know—"

"As soon as the weather clears Raina will be moved to a larger medical facility." She coolly interrupted his babbling. "It will be a few days before she can fly home."

"I don't *have* a few days," he said, his relief turning into a frown. "I need to get home."

Eve struggled not to let her contempt or her temper show. It was hard not to judge a man who willingly left his wife in order to have a romantic tryst in the South Pacific with his mistress and then abandoned her among strangers when he had no more use for her.

But when he gave a long exhalation and had the grace

to look uncomfortable Eve realized she hadn't been successful in concealing her feelings.

"You know."

She didn't pretend to misunderstand.

"Your relationship with Raina isn't my concern," she said coolly. "Her health and recovery is." She was silent for a few moments before adding quietly, "She needs emotional as well as physical recovery time, Mr. Greenway. I hope you do the right thing."

Without waiting for his reply she turned and left, heading back to the OR at a fast clip.

Jasmine looked up when she shoved open the door, her eyebrows rising up her forehead at the sight of Eve's face. "I take it that didn't go well?"

"He's…he's an ass," Eve snarled, having too much respect for the older woman to say exactly what she thought of Mark Greenway. "Do you know he was so relieved she's no longer pregnant that he didn't even ask how she is? Or if he could see her?"

Jasmine patted her arm. "He *is* an insensitive ass," she agreed. "But not all men are so quick to abandon their responsibility once the fun is over."

Eve just sighed, not wanting to upset the other woman by disagreeing. Of course she knew that not all men were alike. She just hadn't had personal experience with any other kind.

It always made her think that maybe there was something wrong with her. With her family. Maybe the Carmichael women were cursed—destined always to choose the wrong kind of man. The kind who would abandon them once their fun wasn't so much fun anymore.

But not Eve. She would rather be alone than find herself as the "other woman." No man, she reminded herself firmly, was worth the utter devastation that they left behind.

She just had to convince her sister of that.

CHAPTER EIGHT

EVE BECAME AWARE of the roaring sounds beyond the hospital walls. Something heavy thudded against the building and she jumped, flashing a nervous look toward the door when windows and shutters rattled violently.

The lights flickered. It sounded like all hell had broken loose.

Jasmine, placing instruments in sterilization trays, sent Eve a reassuring glance. "Wind," she explained. "Sounds like a one-fifty."

Eve didn't reply, thinking it sounded like an out-of-control freight train barreling toward them. Everything rattled and banged, and when there was an ominous creak overhead she half expected the roof to go flying off into the night.

Since there was little chance of her making it back to the resort, she might as well be useful.

"Do you need help?"

Stripping off her surgical gown, Jasmine lifted her head to smile at Eve.

"You offering?"

"If you'll have me."

"Then, yes," the older woman said decisively, shrugging into a lab coat. "I just received news that rescuers are bringing in casualties. Apparently a few yachts in the marina found their way into some sitting rooms along the waterfront. From what I hear we need all the help we can get—although I doubt there'll be too many gynecological cases."

Eve grinned, relieved to have something to do. "I'm sure I can remember my ER training."

Jasmine's dark eyes gleamed with amusement. "It's a bit like sex." She laughed. "You never forget how."

Considering how long *that* had been for Eve, she was afraid she *had* forgotten. Oh, not working in the ER. She could probably do *that* in her sleep.

Just as they stepped through the doors to the ER the world outside lit up for a brief instant and then exploded, the resounding boom shaking the building. One second they had lights—the next it was pitch-black.

Eve froze, seeing a whole lot of nothing. Worse, she wasn't familiar with the layout of the hospital and was afraid she'd fall over something or—*oh, God*—someone if she so much as breathed.

There was a moment of utter silence, then the disembodied voice of Jasmine Tahuru muttered a heartfelt, "Dammit."

Eve reached out tentatively and hissed her relief when her hand encountered cool plaster. Carefully edging closer to the wall, she pressed back against it. All the better to face whatever came her way.

There was muted murmuring and footsteps, and then a loud clatter, followed by cursing. The resultant laughter was a little nervous, but it served to cut the thick tension.

"For heaven's sake, everyone, stay where you are until I find some lamps," Jasmine ordered loudly. "We have enough casualties coming in without adding anymore."

Something clicked close by, and a thin beam of light sliced through the inky blackness.

Eve watched as the blade-thin beam moved away. There was the sound of a door opening and the beam disappeared, swallowed by the dark.

She felt utterly alone.

And kind of spooked by the sounds of breathing.

It was creepy—especially when jagged flashes of lightning lit up her surroundings for a split second. She heard a collective sucking-in of breath, as though everyone was waiting for the resultant boom.

It soon came—accompanied by a prickling sensation on the back of her neck. Goose bumps broke out and she sucked in a calming breath, wondering why she felt so on edge. Almost as though she knew something was about to hap—

And then...*there*...behind her...came a stealthy scrape of a shoe on linoleum, the brush of fabric. Heart surging into her throat, she spun around, wishing she had one of those big-ass syringes, or maybe a scalpel—and abruptly come up against a hard wall of muscle.

At that moment lightning flashed briefly, and the huge shadow looming over her had her reacting instinctively. Okay, so it might also have been leftover memories of her childhood—bumping into her mother's men in the middle of the night—or watching too many horror movies, but she gave a strangled gasp and lurched backward, intending to escape.

Hard hands shot out, closing over her upper arms and keeping her from falling on her ass. The next instant a hard, warm body had the same grateful ass pressed up against the wall—along with every other part of her.

With a startled squeak she instinctively brought her knee up—before she recognized the body preventing her from sliding to the floor. Fortunately he reacted just as swiftly, and twisted to prevent a ground-zero touchdown. Her knee grazed his thigh instead.

A pained grunt and a muffled "Dammit..." filled her ears as a warm, familiar masculine scent filled her head.

She sagged in relief. After a couple beats he released her shoulders to flatten his hands against the wall beside her head. Probably to keep himself from wrapping them around her throat.

It would have been a little alarming to be so attuned to someone she'd only known two days if her relief hadn't rendered her so weak.

"Chase?"

His head dipped and the rasp of his stubble scraped the side of her face, setting in motion a full-body shiver that tightened her nipples and sent heat arrowing into secret places. Secret places that hadn't seen any action in forever and were still humming with unfulfilled tension.

His voice was a rough slide of sin and irritation against her tightly strung nerves.

"Expecting someone else?"

She huffed out a nervous laugh, unaware that she was clutching his shirt in tight fists. "I wasn't expecting *any-one*," she lied breathlessly. "And certainly not sneaking up on me."

He gave a soft snort against her neck, as if he suspected she was lying. The feel of his warm breath on her skin had goose bumps marching across her flesh and heading for parts unknown.

Almost as if he knew what he was doing to her, Chase dipped his head and licked her ear. "I wasn't sneaking," he murmured, blowing on the wet spot. It drew a little gasp of pleasure from her throat and sent her nipples into a frantic happy dance of anticipation. "For a city girl, you're certainly oblivious to your surroundings."

"What's that supposed to mean?"

"It means you should be aware of people sneaking up on you."

"I thought you weren't."

"Is that why you tried to knee me in the nuts?"

Her head swam. She really had no intention of discussing his…nuts. "Why are we having this conversation?"

"Maybe I'm trying to distract you from freaking out."

"I'm not freaking out," she whispered defensively.

His voice was a low, amused rumble against the pulse in her neck. "Is that why your heart is pounding?"

Her heart was pounding because he was so damn close she couldn't breathe. Close enough that an idea wouldn't be able to pass between them—although her body was getting *plenty* of ideas. And, *dammit*, he was close enough that she was an inch away from burying her nose in his throat and inhaling his amazing scent.

"My heart is pounding because one minute I was alone and the next you were there. I thought you were a hatchet-wielding psycho."

"Who says I'm not?" he murmured, sliding his big hands to her waist. "Maybe I'm a serial killer who terrorizes the islands, flying off to the next stop before I'm caught."

Her snicker turned into a gasp when he spread his fingers to span her torso, sending heated shivers spreading throughout her body. She recalled in perfect detail the way they'd felt on her naked skin—rough and exciting. She felt a shudder move through her and bit her lip against the moan rising up her throat.

"Then—" she gasped "—I...I g-guess I should w-warn you that I have a b-black belt." *Really? She was stuttering now?* "So...so maybe you should b-back off," she growled a little fiercely. "Before I...before I—"

He gave a low, sexy chuckle and slid his hand beneath her scrubs top to rasp erotically against her belly. She jolted and nearly melted into a puddle at his feet. Darn, but the man had magical hands.

"Before you what?" he murmured, nuzzling the sensitive spot just beneath her ear. She licked her lips and tried to focus on their conversation, wondering why her muscles weren't obeying the command from her brain to shove him away. "Before I...um..."

What the heck were they talking about?

"Before you rip off my clothes?" he murmured helpfully,

chuckling when she gulped noisily. "Have your wicked way with my sexy body?"

She gave a strangled snort, but her body was happy to comply with his suggestion. And to make matters worse a little voice in the back of her mind begged, *Oh, yes. Can we? Please.*

"I was thinking more along the lines of drawing blood," she said breathlessly. "You know—check for tropical diseases? I hear there are some pretty rare ones that can wreck your…um…well, your love life."

"You're a little bloodthirsty, you know that?" he murmured, not sounding particularly perturbed by her threat. "But my love life?" He chuckled. "It's just fine. Wanna check it out, Doc?"

She was on the verge of saying, *No, thank you,* when the lights flickered and an amused voice filled the heated silence.

"Wow," Jasmine Tahuru said dryly. "Maybe we should hit the lights again. No telling who'll show up next time."

For a breathless beat Eve's eyes collided with Chase's. There was something in the look he sent her that had the backs of her knees sweating—and a hot ball of something that felt very much like panic cramping her stomach.

Where was a good earthquake when you needed one? Or lightning and thunder, for that matter? And what the heck had happened to her self-control?

"So," she gulped through a tight throat, facing their audience while trying to pretend she *hadn't* been about to be kissed senseless. "What would you like me to do first?"

She smoothed her hair off her face with shaking hands, painfully aware of Chase standing behind her. It seemed even the air molecules separating them were supercharged with heat, sizzling with a primal awareness she'd never experienced.

The shocking truth was that he only had to come near her and every strand of her DNA went berserk.

"I'm putting you in charge," Jasmine said briskly. "Until I find out what's wrong with the generator."

"I'll deal with the generator," Chase said, sounding amused. "Sounds like you'll have enough on your hands soon."

His words had no sooner emerged than the ER door banged open, bringing in both the storm and their first casualties.

"I hope you're good with your hands," Jasmine said striding forward. "It can be a little temperamental."

"I'm *very* good with my hands," Chase assured her, but he looked at Eve. The heat almost had her brand-new panties melting off her body.

Jasmine snorted. "I'll just bet you are."

Rattled, Eve was about to join her when one of those large fists grabbed her scrubs top and pulled her back against him. The contact lasted only a brief second, but the sensation of his hard chest echoed through her body like a howl in the Grand Canyon.

Eve sent a wild-eyed look over her shoulder at him, thinking she'd likely be safer out there. In the storm.

"Don't go anywhere," he growled. "*Especially* not out there."

"You are not the boss of me," she managed, over a tight, dry-as-desert throat. "Besides, what about you?"

"I'm a big boy," he said shortly, and turned on his heel. "I can handle myself."

Oh, yeah, Eve thought, watching his broad back disappear around the corner. He certainly was. A big boy, that was. But she was a big girl too, she reminded herself fiercely. She could handle anything as well as him—if not better.

Couldn't she?

Abruptly aware of a little niggle of doubt, she promptly squared her shoulders. Of course she could. She'd handled med school, three jobs *and* her needy family. If she could do

all that without breaking a sweat she could handle one su-
persexy grumpy pilot with her hands tied behind her back.

No sweat.

Chase was glad to have something to do. Hospitals gave
him the willies and he usually did everything and anything
to stay out of them.

He was also rattled by what had just happened. Or
what he'd allowed to happen…in a crowded ER and with
a woman he wasn't sure he even liked.

He'd clearly lost his mind, because he just had to be near
her and when he was, his body took over. That had never
happened before. Not even with his ex.

Dr. Tahuru's son Henri, a civil engineering student helping out during his vacation, took him to the building that
housed the generator. For an hour the two of them tinkered
and sweated in the torchlight, managing—briefly—to re-
suscitate the generator by banging on the motor with a
wrench. It didn't fix the problem but it did make Chase
feel better. Marginally.

Finally he opened the fuel line and found it clogged with
dirt. *Yep.* No wonder it sounded like an asthmatic, geriatric
smoker with a heart problem.

This necessitated a full inspection of the motor, which he
did by taking it apart. It was antiquated, to say the least, and
looked like it hadn't had a good service in years. The cool-
ing and exhaust system was clogged with dust and debris.

Chase cleaned the filter, surprised that it hadn't seized
years ago. He also opened and cleaned the piston shafts,
sending Henri to look for lubricant.

After replacing the spark plugs and flushing the fuel
line he put everything back together, waiting with bated
breath as Henri flipped the switch.

The generator gave a couple pathetic shudders before it
kicked in and settled to a noisy humming. After a few tense
seconds the lights flickered, brightened and finally held.

The two men shared a grin and a fist bump before securing the building and dashing back through the torrential rain. Chase headed back to the tiny ER and watched the controlled chaos for a while, marveling at the sight of Dr. Eve Carmichael in her element.

And she *was* in her element, even though she looked nothing like the snooty, well-groomed big-city professional who'd swooned at his feet two days ago.

Dressed in light blue scrubs accessorized with a stethoscope, and with her hair escaping a high ponytail, she looked both capable and somewhat rumpled. It was a look he found he liked. It made her appear younger...softer... and when she looked up and their eyes locked across the room that glowing amber gaze felt like a one-two blow to the chest.

Whoa! he thought. He wasn't sure if it was the sharp intelligence or the flash of vulnerability that had made his head reel and his chest ache.

Dammit. Did she know that he was genetically incapable of resisting vulnerability? Cool, remote and uptight he could resist. But she'd had to go and change on him. Becoming warm, soft and vulnerable.

He scoffed at himself. He was imagining things. There was nothing helpless about this fancy specialist from Boston.

Turning away, he shoved shaking hands through his hair. "Hey."

At the softly spoken word right behind him, he glanced over his shoulder into her serious eyes. And *damn* if she wasn't suddenly the most beautiful women he'd ever seen. Even bruised and battered, and dressed in baggy scrubs, she took his breath away.

"Hey," he said back lamely, unable to think of a single smart-ass comment. Her eyes were strangely intent, running over him as if she expected to see new injuries.

"You okay?"

Unable to tear his gaze from hers, he lifted a hand to scratch his jaw. He'd shaved hours ago and the sound rasped into the awkward silence. "Yeah—you?"

She blinked, clearly startled by the question, and Chase had to wonder if anyone ever took the time to ask her if *she* was okay.

She angled her head, looking amused. "Of course I'm okay. I'm always okay."

Arching his eyebrow, he said softly, "Always?" And when the smooth skin between her brows wrinkled in confusion he had to fold his arms across his chest to keep from reaching out to smooth it away. "Well…" he mused. "Just yesterday you were afraid you'd die before you had a screaming orgasm. You definitely weren't okay then."

Wild color surged beneath her skin and right before his eyes she became all flustered annoyance, heading for up-tight. And, although he welcomed that flash of irritation, he wondered at the constant need he had to nudge her off balance.

"I can't believe you brought that up," she accused, spinning away. Laughing, he grabbed her scrub top and drew her back against him when she would have stomped off.

Yeah, well, the only reason he'd brought it up was to divert her from those soft looks of concern. Concern he didn't know what to do with. It made his chest ache and the back of his skull tighten.

But, hey, imagine that… It had worked. He was diverted. She was diverted. Mission accomplished.

With a growl, she wrenched herself free and he let her go, his gaze dropping to that world-class ass as she hurried off. Unfortunately it was hidden beneath the baggy scrubs, but that didn't stop his mind wandering into dangerous territory.

He'd had a narrow escape earlier and he assured himself that he wasn't thinking about getting another up-close-and-personal view of that part of her anatomy. Or any other part.

It had been a mistake. Besides, she was only here to mess up his brother's life. He had no intention of letting her mess up *his*. Been there, done that. He just wished certain parts of his damn anatomy would receive the message too.

CHAPTER NINE

IT WAS NEARLY two in the morning when Chase let himself into the hotel suite. He was wet, steaming mad and, he had to admit, struggling to remain calm. Especially when he found the suite empty and no sign that she'd been there.

There was also no sign that anyone *else* had been there either. With her.

Hissing out air through his clenched teeth, he shoved his hands through his dripping hair, thoroughly disgusted with himself.

His marriage had been over a long time and he'd been over it even longer. But he clearly wasn't over himself. Because the combination of mad panic and disgust had left him with a ball of fire in his gut and a tight, hollow sensation in his chest. It reminded him of a time in his life he wanted to forget and cranked up his irritation into the red zone. He'd left that life far behind, and in the five years he'd been in the South Pacific not once had he experienced that gnawing, angry helplessness.

Until *she'd* dropped into his life, with her tawny hair and 100-percent-proof whiskey gaze, turning his carefully constructed life upside-freaking-down. It was no wonder he was stomping around like an idiot without GPS.

After leaving her in the ER he'd joined the rescue effort and spent the next few hours helping out. At least until the wind had dropped to thirty knots and the island had no longer been in danger of being blown away. It was still pouring with rain like a rerun of Noah's flood, but they'd finally managed to evacuate everyone from the marina.

With nothing to do but wait for morning he'd returned to the hospital, filthy, elated, and sporting a few more scrapes and bruises than he'd had that morning. Along with his elation there had been an odd impatience to see a certain sexy doctor, with visions of escorting her back to the hotel and—

Yeah. Fine. So the *and* had been a little X-rated. Sue him. He was a guy on the edge and the thought of that *and* had had him steam-drying in seconds. That was until he'd found out that Jasmine Tahuru had sent Henri to take her back to the hotel over an hour earlier—and hadn't returned.

His blood had promptly turned to ice as he'd imagined all kinds of scenarios. Okay, so he wasn't exactly proud of that first scenario—of Eve and the young student locked in passion—but then an even worse image of a giant wave swallowing them whole, or Henri crashing into a downed tree, had popped front and center, sending dread slicing through him.

He'd torn out of the hospital as though his ass was on fire. But hadn't come across a crashed vehicle. Or signs that a car had gone off the cliff either. And then a slow boil had started in his gut. He'd told himself he'd find her fast asleep in their bed—alone—and that he'd laugh at his stupid-ass thoughts.

Only now, he realized, checking out the empty bathroom, he was the one alone.

Uh-huh. Story of his life.

He glared at the empty bed for so long a puddle of rainwater formed around his feet and he swung away, a sound of disgust finding its way past his lips.

What the hell had he expected? Her waiting in the bed? Candlelight flickering across her soft naked skin? Her smiling softly as she waited for him to join her?

He snorted rudely at his own lame imagination and

then a sound outside the door had him spinning around. It banged open, revealing Eve backing into the room and nudging the door closed with her hip. She turned, and instead of seeing her arms wrapped around the young stud—*yeah, yeah, he was an idiot*—he saw they were filled with a tray piled high with food and an open bottle of wine.

He knew the instant she saw him. She came to an abrupt halt, a loud gasp escaping her lips. "*Ohmigod!* Chase?"

Her eyes widened to dinner plates. He opened his mouth and took a step toward her, but she gave a gasping squeak and backed up, bumping into the entrance hall table.

Dishes rattled loudly and began to topple. Acting on instinct, he grabbed the tray just as it began to slip from her shaky grasp.

Well, hell. "Yeah, it's me," he all but snarled. "Who the hell *else* would it be?"

She slapped a hand to her chest and gasped. "*Dammit. You have got* to stop *doing* that." Her wide eyes took him in with one sweeping look, as if to make sure it really was him, then she sagged against the table, eyes closed, her breath whooshing in and out like she was practicing for the labor ward.

After she had her breathing under control she opened her eyes to glare at him. "What…what the heck were you doing? Steam-drying? You scared the bejesus out of me."

He was steaming, all right, and about to blow a gasket. But for a minute longer he just stared at her, drinking in her rumpled, flushed appearance. The anger warred with relief at seeing her unharmed, and it made him feel a little sick—and a lot unbalanced.

He wondered inanely if he'd finally cracked.

Yeah. No way was he answering that question.

He was just about to shove her up against the nearest wall when he realized he was still holding the tray. Casting his gaze around irritably, he gave a muttered curse and dumped the whole lot on the floor, catching the wine at the last instant.

Still crouched, he caught movement out of the corner of his eye and looked up to see her edging along the wall, watching him like he was a large and hungry predator about to pounce.

Yeah, well. He *felt* like pouncing. And there'd be no avoiding him. Not this time.

She froze, looking like a deer caught in the headlights— a realization that had dark satisfaction adding to the volatile mix of emotions making him a little crazy.

Smart move, lady.

For a long moment they remained frozen, until she expelled air in a long hiss of annoyance.

Feeling more than a little annoyed himself, he rose and stepped closer. Okay, he *stalked*, and he had the satisfaction of seeing her blink uncertainly at him. And when he pushed her a little roughly up against the wall and caged her between his arms she gaped up at him like he'd grown two heads.

Yeah, well, that's what you get for acting crazy.

"What—what are you doing?"

He leaned forward and cursed the warm, heady scent hijacking his senses. His head spun. Whether it was from the smell of the food on the tray or her, he wasn't sure, but it ratcheted his annoyance factor up a couple hundred notches.

"Do you *know* what I've just been through?" he grated softly in her ear.

She nudged him back to check him over, and when she made a low sound of concern he knew she'd found his new scrapes and bruises. But he didn't want her concern, *dammit*. He wanted—

"You're hurt?" She interrupted his thoughts with soft words and soft hands cupping his face. "Why didn't you say something?"

Grinding his back teeth together, he ignored the urge to rub his face against her soft palms.

What a sap.

"Forget about that," he growled impatiently. "I'm fine." *Uh-huh.* "I thought…" He hissed out a breath and the words rasped through the heated silence. "I thought I told you not to leave the hospital."

Oh, yeah. That should go down well with Ms. Independence.

She instantly stiffened, sucking in a furious breath. Her shove was no longer a nudge, and the light of battle was sparking a golden fire in her eyes. Being the ass he was, he decided he liked it. *A lot.*

Hoping to annoy her further, he crowded her between the wall, the hall table and his body, and was rewarded by a soft growl and a hard shove.

Oh, yeah, that's more like it, he thought with a savage grin. *Bring it on, lady. Let's rumble.*

"I don't answer to *you*, you arrogant ass," she hissed furiously, reminding him that he was mad about something too.

Oh, right.

"I went back to the hospital," he gritted through clenched teeth. "And when Dr. Tahuru said you'd left hours ago with Henri I couldn't help imagining him losing control and driving you both off a damn cliff."

Okay, so he'd imagined other stuff too, but he didn't have to tell her that. He was stupid, but not *that* stupid.

She instantly stilled, and the tension thickened until he could have practically hacked at it with a broadsword. He dipped his head to see her eyes and found that potent whiskey gaze an inch away from his, confused and wary. She slowly slid a pacifying hand up his abs to his chest and patted him.

Like he needed *soothing*, for God's sake.

His muscles turned to stone, rippling beneath her long

fingers and warm palm. And *damn* if it didn't soothe and electrify him all at once.

"I'm sorry you were worried," she said carefully. "But, as you can see, I'm fine." A shoulder hitched helplessly. "I was starving, so we raided the kitchen."

"We...?"

"Me and Henri. His uncle is the chef here."

Exhaling explosively, Chase dropped his forehead to the wall beside hers and wondered idly if *everyone* on this damn island was related. It was a stupid thing to think in the circumstances, but with his body resting against her trembling form he needed a moment.

Oh, wait. That was *him*. *He* was the idiot trembling like a little kid after a terrifying nightmare.

Disgusted with himself, he pushed away from the wall and turned, shoving a hand through his wet hair. Droplets of water scattered everywhere.

What the hell was wrong with him? It wasn't like he *wanted* to be responsible for her. He didn't. He was *relieved*. Relieved she didn't expect more from him than a way to reach her sister.

Which was fine. *So freaking damn fine.*

Rattled by his internal chaos, he turned back to find her eyes locked on him, wary and a little confused. *Yeah, well, join the club.* He was confused too.

He'd clearly lost his mind.

Realizing he needed to put a little distance between them before he did something stupid, he moved away.

"So where *is* young Henri?"

In the pause he could practically hear her eyebrows rising up her forehead. "Eating ice cream, probably."

He gave a snort and sent a look over his shoulder. She'd folded her arms beneath her breasts and her narrow-eyed look told him louder than words that he was an idiot.

His mouth twisted. *Tell me something I don't know, lady.*

With an irritated sound in the back of her throat she tried

to move—shove past him—but he wasn't ready to let her go so he just shifted, neatly blocking her escape. And nearly smiled when she stopped abruptly with a loud exhalation.

"Look," she said.

She was getting annoyed again—and why he found that hot, he didn't know. But he was hanging on to his sanity by his last nerve and couldn't be held responsible for his actions.

"I'm sorry you were worried," she said with exaggerated politeness, "but I've been taking care of myself for a long time. Besides—" she shrugged "—you'd disappeared, and I didn't think you'd care what I did."

"Why the hell wouldn't I care?" he demanded, feeling a little insulted by this slur on his character.

Her quick look of surprise left a crease of confusion between her brows. As though she wasn't used to anyone caring.

Scowling, he lifted a hand to rub at the sudden ache in his chest. An ache that had appeared at the notion that she didn't expect anyone to care. Then again, maybe he was having a mild coronary. Maybe he should get her to check him out.

She was a doctor, wasn't she?

His gaze swept over the damp, rumpled scrubs, molded to her very fine body.

Yep. Good idea.

And an even better idea would be to do it naked.

He reached over his head, grabbed a handful of the wet cotton between his shoulders and yanked the shirt over his head. Then he kicked off his sneakers and reached for his jeans.

"What are you doing?"

A glance in her direction caught her shocked gaze locked on his fingers. She was wildly flushed. A dangerous heat gathered low in his belly. A heat that had been growing steadily since she'd passed out at his feet. It would have been all the more precarious because of his dangerous mood if he hadn't begun to enjoy himself.

What that said about him, he didn't know. Or particularly care. There was only one thing on his mind.

Okay, two.

One: get naked.

Two: get Eve naked.

Things would get pretty interesting from there.

"I'm taking off my clothes."

Her eyes widened at the sound of his zipper filling the tense silence. She looked a little panicked. "I... You... *What?*" She gulped. "Aren't you um…hungry?"

He paused to study her in the low lamplight, taking in her heightened color and the tight nipples pressing against the thin damp cotton of her scrubs top. Her fascinated gaze was sliding all over his chest, arrowing down to his gaping jeans as though she couldn't make up her mind what she wanted to lick first.

His lips twitched. "Oh, yeah…" he drawled softly. He had several ideas about where she could start. "I'm starved."

Her eyes jerked upward and, on seeing his expression, narrowed to slits. She growled. Actually growled. And since he couldn't help himself, he smirked.

"Chase—" she began, trying to sound firm and patient, as though about to explain to a preadolescent why he couldn't smoke weed.

"Eve?" he mocked softly.

Rolling her eyes, she made a wild gesture with her arm. "What is…this?"

"This?"

"Yeah…*this.*"

He raised an eyebrow. "You're…wet," he murmured silkily, coming to a stop barely an inch away.

She gaped at him, her face flushing bright red. "I'm… *wha-a-at?*"

Suppressing a chuckle at her misinterpretation of his words, he leaned close. "Yep. And you need to undress."

"I…no…I do not," she spluttered, gripping the scrubs top between her breasts.

"Uh-huh. You can't shower in your clothes."

She paused, narrowed her eyes. "Shower…?"

His mouth twitched at the wary expression that turned hunted when he leaned closer. "Yeah," he murmured in her ear. "Sh-o-w-er." He let that sink in as he straightened. "What did you think I meant?"

"Um…nothing…"

He grinned and settled his hands on her hips. She jumped, tensing even more when he gripped her scrubs top and began to lift it up her torso. Squirming, she slapped at his hands, so he transferred them to her soft skin instead.

"S-stop that," she gasped, wriggling, her breath catching as his palms slid up her sides. "I mean…um…"

He bent his knees to look her in the eye. "You have something to say, Doctor?"

She tried to appear unconcerned as she continued to tug on his hands. "This is a…a mistake."

"I beg to differ."

"It *is*," she insisted, practically shooting his blood pressure through the top of his head when she nibbled nervously on her lip.

He wanted to do that, dammit. He had plans to do it—as well as nibble on other very delicious parts of her anatomy.

"Angry sex is *always* a mistake."

He froze. "Angry…?" He gaped at her, insulted that she would think him capable of that. He nearly stepped away, but one look at her face told him she was as aroused as he was.

He pressed his thigh into the notch of her thighs. She sucked in a sharp breath, and by the way her pupils dilated he knew it wasn't just because his jeans were cold and wet.

"This is I-want-to-jump-your-bones sex," he explained

with a growl. "This is if-I-don't-have-you-now-I'm-going-to-explode sex."

She looked like she didn't know whether to be flattered or insulted. "So…you're not angry?"

He pressed his erection against her. "Does this feel like I'm angry?"

She made a sound in the back of her throat—kind of a mix between a squeak and a husky laugh that shouldn't have been sexy but was.

"Chase."

"Eve." He said it with a smile in his voice. But his amusement faded when he saw the look in her eye. Kind of aroused and terrified all at once. "Dammit," he cursed, moving back a couple inches. "I'm not angry and I won't hurt you. Tell me you know that?"

She rolled her eyes. "I know that. It's just…"

"Just what?

She gave a huge sigh and muttered something beneath her breath. Her gaze slid away, not quite meeting his.

He cocked an eyebrow, wondering if he'd heard right. "What was that?"

Color stained her cheekbones. "It's been a long time," she repeated loudly, looking flustered.

"A long time?" he echoed distractedly, momentarily pre-occupied with her mouth. Especially when she licked her lip and left it shiny and damp. His mouth watered.

Oh, man.

"Since…what?"

She huffed out an incredulous laugh and gave him a hard shove. Her death look was answer enough.

"That's okay," he said, laughing at her. Laughing at himself. "I think I remember enough for both of us." Then he whipped her top over her head and tossed it somewhere behind him, not caring where it landed.

Beneath the scrubs top was a teeny-tiny crop top. And no bra. As evidenced by the way thin, tight fabric molded to her full, naked breasts. Breasts, he discovered as his breath whooshed out, that were either cold or really...*really* happy to see him.

Seeing the direction of his gaze, Eve gave a mortified squeak and slapped her hands over her breasts.

"Didn't you want to...um...shower?" she asked desperately.

His lips twitched, but she was too busy sliding her gaze over his chest like he was a five-course meal to notice. "Uh-huh." He was only interested in dessert.

"But...but I'm starving."

"Yeah..." he breathed, his fingers caressing her naked shoulders, and he was gratified to see goosebumps erupting beneath his touch. Holding her gaze, he drawled, "Me too."

"S-stop that," she gasped, waving her arm desperately. "Maybe what you n-need is a c-cold shower. A *really* cold shower."

He grinned and caught her flapping hand to lace his fingers with hers. "Nuh-uh," he said firmly, dropping his gaze to the tight nipples clearly outlined in damp white cotton. "There'll be no cold showers tonight." He turned to the bathroom and tugged on her hand. "What you need is a steaming...*hot*...experience."

She gulped. "S-steaming?" She looked a bit dazed, a lot aroused. "Hot?"

"Uh-huh." He nodded, eyeing the shower stall to gauge if they would both fit. He was a big guy, and he took up a lot of room, but since he didn't intend to let her get too far away from him he reckoned they'd manage just fine.

He pulled her all the way into the bathroom and closed the door, barring her escape. Then he slid his hands around her hips and shoved both scrub pants and panties down her legs.

Her eyes, slumberous and dark as old gold, shimmered in the soft light. And when she just looked at him, once more sending his blood pressure shooting through the top of his head, he took her hand and put it on his shoulder.

She leaned on him as he helped her step out of her clothing. Then, rising to his feet, he swept the little crop top over her head, leaving her naked.

Oh, man. She was hotter than a bushel of jalapeños.

Conscious only of the storm brewing inside the bathroom, Chase and Eve silently regarded each other, each waiting for the other to make the next move.

Deciding it would have to be him, Chase reached behind her, opened the stall and flipped on the water. The abrupt sound was startling in the heated silence. A silence that cocooned them in intimacy, isolating them from the rest of the world. It was just them. Here. Now.

By tomorrow he would have her out of his system and he could go back to his peaceful life.

He opened his mouth to tell her that he wasn't interested in anything more than one night when she beat him to it, cupping his face in her hands.

"I'm leaving," she said, so intently that he paused, confused. And, he had to admit, shocked.

"What? *Now?*"

She gave a low, husky laugh and his IQ shrank another hundred points. "Soon," she said much to his relief. "I just want you to know that…that…"

"That what?"

Her gaze caught and held his. "That this is a one-time thing. Brought on by…circumstances."

He tried not to feel offended, since he'd been thinking the same thing, and just said, "You mean the result of adrenaline and sharing something intense, like surviving a plane crash?"

A strange emotion flittered across her face too fast for Chase to identify. "Yes, something like that."

He held her gaze for a moment longer and then decided

not to waste any more time arguing. "Are we finished talking now?"

She blinked at him, then huffed out a surprised laugh. "Yes. We're finished talking."

Her breathing was ragged and uneven, and it was a moment before he realized that his was too. With relief and renewed lust.

Thank God she's not planning on leaving right now, nor expecting anything beyond sunrise.

Her hands wandered over his damp flesh to the waistband of his jeans and he forgot to think.

"So, then, why are you still dressed?"

"Maybe..." he rasped hoarsely, feeling her touch like a brush of living fire across his skin. "Maybe you should do something about it."

After a long moment her eyes dropped past his mouth and moved down his tight throat before sliding hungrily over his chest to where his jeans gaped.

At her sharply inhaled breath he looked down and realized he was so big and hard—bigger and harder than he'd ever been—that his erection was pushing the zip and plackets aside.

His chuckle was a rusty sound, low in his throat. "Looks like I'm just as happy as you."

"Me?"

"Oh, yeah." He brushed the backs of his fingers against one tight nipple and nearly combusted at her soft murmur of hunger.

In that instant any control he might have had vanished.

With a growl of impatience he tugged her to him, shuddering when her soft breasts and hard nipples flattened against his chest. The contact made a mockery of his famed control and he turned, backing her into the stall, covering her gasp with his mouth as he followed her in.

The kiss instantly heated, and before it sucked him under

he remembered to reach behind him and fumble the door closed.

The next few minutes were a battle of hands and mouths and tongues. Chase was so hard it was painful. Especially when she wriggled against him like she couldn't get close enough. His eyes literally crossed in his head and his knees buckled.

Before he could regain control of his legs—or his mind—Eve had pushed him to the built-in seat and climbed into his lap. Her soft wet heat pressed against his erection and he just about shot off into space.

Cursing, and breathing like a steam engine chugging up a mountain pass, he grabbed her hips and held her away from ground zero—before he exploded and things ended before they'd even had a chance to begin. Besides, he had plans that would hopefully take the rest of the night to fulfil...

CHAPTER TEN

TAKING ADVANTAGE OF the space he'd made between their bodies, Eve reached down and stroked him through the opening of his wet jeans. When she couldn't quite reach all of him—*ohmigod, he was huge*—she slid off his lap and tugged him to his feet, her hands impatient as she shoved the denim over his hips.

"Wait…" Chase chuckled, catching her wrists and tucking them into the small of her back. *"Wait!"* he gasped, his eyes nearly rolling back in his head when the movement arched her back, so her breasts thrust upward and her belly brushed his blue steeler.

She wriggled closer, reveling in the wild look that flashed through his stormy eyes.

"God, Eve. What's…the…rush?"

What's the rush? He was the rush. *This* was the rush. And she was afraid that if they stopped for even a second she'd combust and it would all be over and she'd never get to feel him inside her.

And she needed this…*him*. Really, *really* badly.

Ignoring his rough, barely incomprehensible words, she growled, "You're overdressed," and sank her teeth into the hard muscle of his shoulder.

He hissed out a soft curse and, taking advantage of his distraction, she managed to free one hand—which she used to touch him…finally touch all that long, thick, silky hardness.

"*Dammit*, woman," he ground out, capturing her hand and roughly shoving her up against the wall, where he held her captive. Breathing heavily, he muttered, "At this rate I'll last about two seconds."

Eve licked her lips and lifted her hungry gaze from his open jeans. His smoky eyes burned hellfire bright, and the sheer naked lust in them had her inner muscles clenching convulsively.

Oh, boy. Talk about lasting only two seconds… *Yeesh.* She was a heartbeat away from coming herself. Right. Out. Of. Her. Skin. And he hadn't even touched her good parts yet.

Shocked by the storm of sensation whipping through her, Eve squeezed her eyes tightly closed and at the same time squeezed her inner thighs together. The move only made an explosive orgasm more imminent. She gave a low moan and froze, breathing hard.

With her hands held captive beside her head, hard cold tile at her back and heat pumping off him in waves, Eve felt like a willing sacrifice to the volcano gods. Then, because the waiting was driving her out of her mind, she rocked her hips into him.

And because it felt so darn good she moaned in the back of her throat and did it again.

"Stop," he gritted through clenched teeth.

But when he didn't move away she gave a slow little cat smile and did it again and again, until he growled out a guttural curse and abruptly pushed away.

Feeling light-headed and weak-kneed, Eve watched as Chase shoved the wet denim down to his feet in one violent move. Finally kicking his jeans aside, he straightened and stared at her, a wild, hungry male intent on his next meal.

Eve, determined to feast on him too, pushed away from the wall and stepped into his space. Surprised by her bold move, he stumbled back until his shoulders met resistance. Elated at having *him* backed against the wall for once, Eve grabbed the soap and finally put her hands on his sculpted eight-pack.

Unfortunately he hadn't been caught *that* off-guard. He grunted. "Oh, no, you don't," he said, swiping water from his eyes with one big hand and the soap from her with the other. "If we're going to play all night, *I* get to go first."

Actually, it was Eve who got to go first...then second... and *ohmigod...* By which time she was squeaky clean and limp as a noodle.

Chase quickly soaped and rinsed himself before hitting the controls. The water was abruptly shut off, leaving her wheezing and panting in the sudden silence. Good thing he was wheezing and panting too—for an entirely different reason. She smirked, hungrily eyeing his erection.

Before she could recover he was tugging her out of the shower and wrapping her in a huge fluffy towel.

"Dammit," she murmured weakly, sagging against his wide, damp chest. "I wanted to do that!"

"What? Get the towel?"

His lips twitched, and if she'd been compos mentis she might have interpreted his look as loaded with amused affection.

His next words, "Make yourself come three times?" had her lifting a limp hand to swat at him.

"No," she wheezed. "I wanted to make you lose control."

Through sleepy eyes she saw his mouth curve, and she got a hot flash just remembering where that mouth had been and—*oh, my*—what it was capable of doing.

The hot flash turned into a spark and then—*wow, look at that!*—she was suddenly raring to go for round four.

And considering she'd had the edge taken off—*three times!*—being the one in control sounded like an excellent plan.

She waited until he'd tossed her onto the bed and followed her down, a condom between his teeth.

Quick as a flash she hooked her leg around his and shoved at his shoulder, rolling them both over until she was leaning over him, straddling his hips. At his shocked expression, she smirked down from her lofty height, and then took advantage of his surprise at finding himself on his back to pluck the small foil packet from between his teeth.

Instead of getting all grumpy and alpha, Chase grinned up at her, his eyes gleaming like polished silver between dark spiky lashes. As though amused by her bid for dominance, he stacked his hands under his head like he was relaxing on a South Pacific beach.

We'll see about that, flyboy.

"We gonna play doctor, Doctor?"

His lazy drawl was deep and amused, but Eve was pleased to discover that his heart was pounding beneath her palm like it wanted to leap into her hand.

Ha. He clearly wasn't nearly as cocky as he pretended.

Her gaze dropped to his erection and she did a quick reassessment. *Okaaaay*, so that wasn't quite true. She smirked. He was *very* cocky. And getting cockier the longer she studied him.

She licked her lips, grinning when a low, rough groan emerged from low in his throat. It sounded like the ragged sound of a man on the very edge of control. A control she wanted to shatter.

"No," she murmured gleefully. "We're going to play another kind of game altogether."

His mouth quirked even as his eyes darkened. "Do your worst, Doctor," he invited smugly.

And Eve did.

Eyeing his ripped chest and shoulders, she reached out and drew a teasing line from the center of his chest down the middle of his torso with her fingernail. He hissed out a curse and arched into her caress, jaw tight, muscles straining.

Distracted from her enjoyment at seeing his smug expression fade, Eve thought that he was even more beautiful like this: features tight, eyes glittering and the low lamplight etching his muscles in stark relief.

There were six hundred and forty muscles in the human body and his were…*awesome*. She knew the names of every muscle and she wanted to lick each one as she named it.

Leaning forward, she licked one pectoral and then the other. And then, because the size of his arms fascinated her, she moved there next, muttering each name an instant before she licked first his deltoid, then his tricep, followed by his bicep. Each muscle was rock hard and quivering beneath smooth, damp skin, and tasted so yummy she just had to open her mouth and…bite.

He reacted like he'd been shot. With a savage growl he surged up and quick as lightning reversed their positions. Shocked by the speed at which the tables had been turned, Eve gaped up at him.

"Dammit," she complained breathlessly, fighting the urge to rock into the narrow hips snug between her open thighs. "I…was…*busy*."

His grunted words, "Later…you can play later," sounded almost incomprehensible. He was breathing like he'd just swum around the entire island—underwater. After a few harshly sucked in breaths he confessed, "I'm about two seconds from launching."

Snickering, she gave in to the urge and rocked her hips, watching with fascination as the tendons in his neck stood out in stark relief. His breath whooshed out on a muttered string of curses. But before she could revel in her small victory, Chase had ripped open the packet and protected them with unsteady fingers.

Suitably…uh…suited up, he locked his fierce gaze with hers, laced their fingers beside her head and in one smooth, hard move, thrust home.

Eve felt her eyes roll back in her head. Her breath caught

and her back arched off the bed. *Oh, God.* He was huge, and despite her readiness the sudden invasion—after long abstinence—sent a tiny pinch of pain shooting through her.

He must have felt the small involuntary reaction and he froze. "Sorry," he ground out in her ear. "Just gimme a sec and I'll make it good, I promise."

But Eve was already melting, already feeling more "good" than she'd ever felt in her life. Her inner muscles rippled as they adjusted to his size and he gave a low, rough laugh.

He lifted his head. Blazing gray eyes seemed to see straight through to her soul. Before she could think to panic and hide, he breathed, "Oh, yeah. Just…like…that."

Dizzy with the heated sensations radiating out from her core, Eve brought her knees up to bracket his hips. And… *oh, man*…the movement forced him deeper than anyone had gone before. With lights exploding behind her eyes, it also forced a low wail to her lips.

With a rough laughing groan Chase began to move, his big, brawny body tense and trembling, every one of those muscles she suddenly couldn't remember the name of, straining.

Things got a little out of control then. He dipped his head and kissed her with all the pent-up hunger that had been building over the past few days. And with little thought to the emotions she'd been suppressing for what seemed like a lifetime, Eve responded as though she'd been starving for the taste of him.

His body began to move…over hers…in hers…with a stamina she might have found impressive if she'd been capable of thought. Even though she was desperate to retain some part of herself aloof, Chase drove her right out of her mind.

It was a short trip to the edge of oblivion and beyond. Clutching him with both arms and legs as she leaped right off the edge, she was vaguely aware of Chase following, his breath escaping in a long, low ragged moan of completion.

Chase awoke wrapped in woman. And for a few sleepy seconds he enjoyed the feel of soft feminine flesh pressed against his body. Since his divorce he'd had a few casual hookups, but he'd never, *ever* fallen asleep afterwards. Falling asleep signified an intimacy he didn't want or need.

Not again—and certainly not with a woman who was set to wreck his brother's life. A woman who, by her own admission, was just passing through, and who, much like a comet, would burn anyone in her path. Especially someone caught up in her fiery beauty.

And he *was* caught up, he admitted, as his skin prickled and heated. He was caught up in a giant fist of need that demanded he take her again. And then maybe again. Because, instead of slaking his thirst, the past five hours had made him hungrier than ever. If he didn't have her again— right now—he would explode.

It was that realization that had his heart pounding and his skin breaking out in a cold sweat. Not panic, he hastily assured himself as he eased away from her soft, feminine warmth, but a very strong sense of self-preservation.

Besides, they'd both said that it was a one-time thing. Well, *she* had. But if she hadn't brought it up, he would have. He didn't intend on letting a woman twist him into knots ever again. Leaving now, while she was soft and warm with sleep, was the kindest thing. For both of them.

Yep. Good thinking. Let's go with kind.

He carefully slid off the bed, ignoring the faint sounds of protest from behind him. He froze, racking his brains for an excuse to give her if she woke and demanded to know where he was going. But when her breathing settled again into those soft snuffling sounds he found so damn sexy Chase's breath escaped in a silent whoosh.

Leaving kept things from becoming awkward—kept

things light and uncomplicated. It also kept him from doing something supremely dumb. Like forgetting himself. Like sliding back under her bewitching spell. Like maybe thinking there was something more than one hot night in paradise.

But there wasn't. Could never be. She was like the storm, sweeping through his life and wreaking havoc.

Quickly gathering his duffel bag and his other belongings, Chase headed for the bathroom. Just before he quietly closed the door he caught sight of her snuggling into his pillow, as though seeking his warmth. He paused a moment to take in all those long lovely lines one last time, greedily.

He pulled on his clothes in the dark, knowing exactly why Adam had taken a bite of that apple. If the biblical Eve had had half the fire and sensuality of Evelyn Carmichael, Adam's fate had been sealed the instant he'd looked into her come-sin-with-me eyes.

Heck, Chase had willingly sinned, knowing it was a mistake. He had no idea what it was about her that turned him into a lust-struck idiot, but he wasn't stupid enough to hang around until she crushed his heart.

Shoving everything into the duffel, Chase quietly headed for the nearest exit, eager to get the hell out before he gave in to impulses that would cost him a lot more than a wrecked seaplane.

A price Chase was unwilling to pay.

Eve woke from what could only be described as a dead sleep to find that she was sprawled across the bed in a boneless, satisfied heap.

Naked.

Naked? Alarmed, she lifted her head—*where was her pillow?*—and discovered through bleary eyes and a curtain of tangled hair that she was alone.

Oh, thank God...

But what the heck had hit her? Then she remembered.

Oh, yeah. Chase Gallagher.

Her head plopped weakly back onto the bed and she lay still as the dead until she recalled in high definition exactly how her bones had gone missing.

Chase Gallagher.

She shivered. Sexy, grumpy flyboy had surprised her with his amazing hands…and mouth…and moves—some she'd never heard of, let alone experienced. But when she caught herself grinning and drooling like a crazy person, she groaned and rolled over, blinking in the bright light flooding the room.

Maybe now *wasn't* the time to be thinking of the creative ways he'd used his tongue, but, *boy…* Eve whooshed out a shuddery breath as her body heated and melted. The man certainly knew how to kiss.

Stunned by the events of the night—by what she'd done—Eve lay unmoving until she was startled from her rapidly escalating panic by a knock at the door. Her heart jerked like she'd been given a jolt from a defibrillator and she jackknifed off the bed. The last thing she needed was Chase catching her lying around naked with a stunned, speechless look on her face. He was smug enough about his sexual prowess without her advertising how thoroughly she'd been ravished.

The movement set all of her six hundred and forty muscles protesting. And her head spinning. *Holy cow.* She felt like she'd fallen off a cliff and caught every rock on the way down.

The knock came again, and with a hasty "Coming…" she fumbled around wildly for the sheet, finally locating it—along with all the other bedding—on the other side of the room. How they had got way over there boggled her sleep-deprived mind.

Wrapping herself in soft cotton, she stumbled to the door and was surprised to find a tray containing coffee—

thank you, God—a plate of exotic fruit and a selection of pastries. And a long flat box...

She looked up to thank the hotel employee but found herself alone. Securing the sheet, she lifted the tray and nudged the box into the suite with her foot, bumping the door closed. The suite appeared empty and she wondered idly—okay, not so idly, she admitted sheepishly—where Chase was.

She took everything back to the bed and poured herself a cup of black coffee. With caffeine finally pumping through her system, she lifted the lid off the box. She didn't know what she expected to find, but hidden beneath a cloud of tissue paper was a wraparound dress in soft green, silk underwear—*no, lingerie*, she recalled absently—a pair of strappy sandals in the same soft green, sunglasses, a hair-brush, a collection of cosmetics from a well-known French company and a designer handbag.

She gawked at the contents, all clearly of the highest quality.

What the heck...?

No note?

Oh, yeah, there it was, she realized, spying a folded piece of paper. She fumbled nervously as she opened it, feeling like a swarm of kamikaze humming birds were dive-bombing her insides.

There was no name scrawled at the bottom to identify the sender, but Eve knew it was Chase. Somehow that bold, illegible scrawl could only belong to the sexy flyboy.

One by one the humming birds turned to lead as she scanned the contents. She had to read it three times before the hastily scrawled words finally registered.

> *Hitched a ride to Port Laurent—business with in-surance co. Bill already settled. Al will take you to Tukamumu. Enjoy.*

Enjoy? That was it?

The question was, "enjoy" what? Breakfast? The goodie box? Seeing her sister? Being abandoned? What?

No *Dear Eve.* No *Love, Chase.* No *Thanks for the memorable one-night stand, I'll never forget you.* No *That was amazing. Let's hook up again.* No *Goodbye, have a nice life.*

Blinking away the sudden prick of tears, Eve swallowed the dry lump of humiliation lodged in her throat.

First of all: *What the heck had she expected?*

Second: *Who was Al?*

And third…

Eve froze when it occurred to her that she'd just been spectacularly dumped. In a scrawled, curt-to-the-point-of-rude note. After the most exciting, *hottest* night of her life.

With a strangled whimper she slapped a hand over her mouth. Oh, God—she'd been dumped. In the middle of the South Pacific. With no money, no passport, no air tickets and no clothes. Except for the ones in the box, of course. Designer lables Chase had most likely paid for.

She wondered a little hysterically if he'd chosen the accessories and cosmetics himself.

Trying not to feel like a hooker who'd been paid for services rendered, Eve shoved everything aside and rose. With a hand pressed to the queasy feeling in her belly, she stared unseeingly out the large window; heart pounding and tears burning the back of her tight throat.

Please tell me I haven't just become my mother.

Finally black spots began dancing in front of her eyes and she wondered if she was about to pass out from humiliation. When her chest began to hurt she realized she was holding her breath, and expelled it in one long, shuddery sigh.

Dammit. She was a thirty-year-old professional woman. A medical specialist, for heaven's sake. She was not a frightened ten-year-old, panicking because she'd been abandoned once again with strangers. Besides, even then she'd squared her shoulders and done what was necessary to protect her sister.

But she was alone now—*oh, God, she was alone*—because her twin had found someone else to love. From here on out it would no longer be Eve and Amelia against the world. Just…Eve.

Shoving shaking hands through her tangled hair, she worked on calming her breathing. She didn't have time to stress about the sudden feeling of abandonment, or the growing anger and disgust aimed right at herself. Not only was it childish and ridiculous, she had more pressing problems. Like replacing her passport and credit cards while being thousands of miles from home. And she really, *really* needed to pay Chase back—if only to salvage her ragged pride.

He must have dropped a couple thousand dollars at least, she thought a little hysterically. And that wasn't counting the luxurious accommodation.

An arbitrary thought occurred to her.

How on earth could a pilot who jaunted around the South Seas because it kept him in mai tais afford designer labels? Especially with his main source of income a tangled mess of twisted metal.

Unfortunately, before she could solve the mystery that was Chase Gallagher, the in-house telephone rang. Thinking that maybe he hadn't left without at least a *so long*, Eve shoved aside her disturbing thoughts and answered.

A soft, feminine voice said, "Dr. Carmichael, this is Kimiki from the front desk. The pilot is here to collect you."

Shoulders sagging, Eve assured herself it was fatigue making her throat burn and not disappointment.

She was lying through her teeth. She *was* disappointed. Stupidly, ridiculously disappointed.

And suddenly on the verge of a panic attack at the thought of getting into another aircraft.

"What? *Already?*" She cast around frantically for luggage she didn't have and remembered at the last instant that she was still wearing a sheet. "I…" She gulped, and then managed a strangled, "Never mind. Tell him I'll be out in twenty minutes. Oh, and, Kimiki? Can you please call Dr. Tahuru and find out how the hotel guest I treated yesterday is?"

"Word is she's recovering just fine," Kimiki assured her. "Mr. Chase flew them out early this morning."

"O-oh?" she stuttered with surprise, her fear of boarding another aircraft fading for a moment. "He f-flew them out? Himself?"

"Yes," Kimiki replied. "He bought one of the small seaplanes the resort uses for island tours and left before seven."

He…*bought*? Her mouth dropped open.

"I—I s-see." *Yeah, she saw about as well as she could digest that particular piece of information. Which was… not at all!*

Thoughts whirling, Eve thanked Kimiki and replaced the receiver. Stunned, she sat staring into space as she absorbed the news until one thing became clear. Chase Gallagher had been in such a hurry to get off the island that he'd bought the first available transport out.

Bought?

Who the heck did *that?* Or, more importantly, *who could* afford *to do that?*

Had he left because he'd thought she would make a scene? Cling? Or—her stomach clenched into a hot ball of humiliation—had he left because he didn't want to see her again?

For some reason that last notion felt like a slap in the face. Stupid, considering she'd made it clear that *she* was leaving, implying—no, *insisting*—that it was a one-time thing. Only now she felt sick to her stomach. Because whatever had happened last night felt anything *but* a one-time thing. And also because she suddenly knew how her mother had felt every time the latest man had walked away without looking back.

Determined to reach her usual aloof state, and to ignore her growing self-directed anger, Eve squared her shoulders and headed for the bathroom. She wasn't her mother. She wouldn't fall to pieces and go on a wild spending and drinking spree, and she darned well wouldn't be returning home with a broken heart or having a string of wild affairs to help her get over this one.

She was strong—far stronger than anyone gave her credit for. She was a survivor, and she had survived worse things than being dumped after the best night of her life.

So, even though it felt like the worst personal betrayal, she dressed in the clothes, armed herself with the make-up he'd provided and left the room without a backward glance.

Her South Seas adventure, it seemed, was over. The sun was shining and the island was once again bathed in that otherworldly light and a soft, balmy breeze.

Everything was as it should be.

Everything except...*her.*

But she'd be fine. She *was* fine, she informed herself, swallowing back the hot burn of angry tears. It had been a really rough few days, but it was time to get back to the real reason she was there. Amelia. Once she'd handled that with her usual calm competence she'd be out of here, home, and getting on with her life.

By the time Eve walked into Reception it was empty. Kimiki smiled when she saw her—probably because for the first time Eve didn't look like a castaway survivor. She'd also managed to conceal most of the bruises and her pale terror at the thought of getting on another seaplane.

She knew she looked poised and together, and she thanked her childhood for teaching her to mask her feelings. It was sheer grit and pride that had her following Kimiki's directions to the terrace, where she found the pilot sharing a cozy coffee with the elegant concierge, Sylvie Armand.

"Ah," Sylvie said, rising to her feet with a welcoming smile. "Here's your girl now."

Eve might have thought it an odd thing for someone to say about a stranger if she hadn't been distracted by the way the older woman leaned forward and, with her hand on the man's shoulder, kissed his tanned cheek before walking away.

Looks like I'm not the only one with a thing for flyboys, Eve thought with a sympathetic grimace.

Not that she had a *thing* for Chase, she hastily assured herself. *No freaking way.* That would just be downright emotional suicide. Besides, even if there *had* been a "thing" between them, it was most definitely over.

The pilot rose and shoved his chair back so quickly it nearly toppled over. Cursing softly, he turned and caught it one-handed, his gaze seeking hers. Eve had a brief impression of a fit, tall, youthful-looking man in his fifties before their eyes met. Dismissing the weird skin prickle down the back of her neck as wild imagination and raw nerves at the thought of having to board a seaplane, she thrust out her hand.

"I'm Evelyn Carmichael," she said coolly, to cover her nerves. "Sorry to keep you waiting."

The man's strangely hopeful expression faded to disappointment, almost as though he'd expected her to…what? Recognize him? But that was ridiculous, considering that, other than finding his amber eyes oddly familiar, she'd never seen him before.

His large hand engulfed hers. "Alain Broussard," he murmured, his gaze intent on her face, as though memorizing her features. "I'm very pleased to meet you, Evie."

Evie? The eerie skin prickle occurred again and Eve slid her hand free, feeling more and more freaked out.

What the heck was going on here?

Seeing her expression, he shoved his hands into his pockets. "Forgive me for being familiar," he murmured sheepishly. "Your sister calls you Evie all the time, and I feel as though I know you."

"Th-that's all right. Evie is…um…fine," she murmured politely as a really awful thought occurred to her. There was only one reason her sister would share personal stuff with this man.

Her blood froze.

Oh, God, please, no.

"Are you…? Is she—?" She stopped abruptly and huffed out an embarrassed laugh, feeling unaccountably flustered and horrified.

She'd always known Amelia had daddy issues, but this was ridiculous. The man was old enough to be their *father*, for God's sake. Besides, how did you ask an almost middle-aged man if he was your sister's fiancé without being rude?

Suddenly very glad she'd dropped everything to make this crazy trip, Eve shoved aside her own problems. It was glaringly obvious that Amelia needed her—if only to prevent her from making a really, *really* bad mistake.

Mentally squaring her shoulders, she sent him a narrow-eyed *I've-got-your-number* look and was surprised to see his amber eyes gleaming with an amused affection mixed with yearning.

Affection? Yearning?

What the hell was going on?

"Why don't we talk on the flight to Tukamumu?" he suggested gently. "I know how eager Amelia is to see you."

After a short pause Eve nodded, her stomach cramping, her heart doing somersaults in her chest. So intent was she on her own nerves that she jolted when he settled a hand in the small of her back. Maybe it was only a gallant gesture on his part, but the feel of his warm hand startled and disturbed her.

He must have felt her instinctive withdrawal, because

he dropped his hand immediately and put a little distance between them.

"I know what you're thinking," Alain said quietly, and when Eve looked across her shoulder, she again caught a glimpse of that odd yearning.

But, she reminded herself firmly, his problems weren't hers. *Sheesh*, she had more than enough of her own to deal with. First, she had to get on a seaplane and survive the flight to Tukamumu without freaking out. And second, there was no way in hell she was letting her sister marry a man old enough to be their father.

"I doubt it," she said coolly, struggling against the almost overwhelming urge to escape. But where to? They were on an island, for God's sake. And he had the only transport out.

He must have sensed her turmoil and decided not to press the issue, because once they were in the air he kept his comments to the scenery. Which Eve appreciated as it kept her from hyperventilating.

Fortunately they were soon flying low over a handful of small, densely vegetated islands clustered near a much larger volcanic island. Most of them were connected by long narrow spits of sand edged with delicate lacy surf. Surrounding the islands was a much larger spit of sand, much like a natural moat, that seemed to embrace the little cluster of islands.

It was…*wow*…stunningly beautiful, and it simply boggled her mind to think her sister would call this place home.

"Tukamumu," her pilot yelled, grinning when he saw her stunned expression. "The island closest to it on the leeward side is Rangi-ura—the resort."

She probably looked like she'd been whacked in the head, but she didn't care. Never—not even in her wildest dreams—could she have dreamed up such a pristine setting. Little wonder her sister had fallen under its spell. It was like something out of a romance novel.

"And that island there?" she asked, pointing to the smaller, rockier island farthest away from the main island.

"That's Matariki—privately owned. If you look carefully you can see the house."

Eyes narrowed against the bright sunlight, Eve could just make out a sprawling structure, practically built into the steep jungle-covered terrain. Winding stone steps led down from a wide wooden deck to a pristine beach and a wooden jetty.

"Someone actually *lives* there?" It was like something out of a movie. Not quite real. People in her world didn't own islands in the Pacific. In fact she'd never even met anyone who owned a holiday home in Martha's Vineyard or Cape Cod, let alone a private island.

He nodded, and she was distracted from the odd look he sent her by their low approach over a crystal-clear lagoon. He banked the seaplane and headed straight for the section of beach a short distance from what she guessed from the thatch umbrellas and deck chairs was the hotel grounds.

Eve spotted the house immediately. Set back from the beach, it was surrounded by a lush green lawn and thick jungle foliage. A woman appeared almost at once, and began running awkwardly across the grass toward the beach.

It took Eve only a second to identify her twin. And, despite the wild relief and joy, she was shocked speechless by the sight of her.

Because not only was she waddling like a duck she was—

"*Ohmigod.* She's...*pregnant?*"

CHAPTER ELEVEN

OBLIVIOUS TO THE fact that her voice had risen to a shocked shriek, Eve gaped through the cockpit window at the enthusiastically waving figure.

She finally turned to glare at the man beside her, almost incoherent with stunned fury that he'd taken advantage of a much younger woman desperate for love and affection.

"She's...*pregnant*?"

Alain maneuvered the plane close to the shore before killing the engines. Something in her expression and tone must have registered. "I told her you needed to be prepared. But—" he shrugged helplessly "—she wanted to surprise you."

Eve's jaw flexed as she ground her teeth together. Oh, she was surprised, all right. Try also shocked—*and devastated*—because her sister looked like she was about to pop.

And she hadn't even told her.

Over the years they'd shared everything. First words, first teeth, first steps. They'd confided in each other about dates and their first sexual encounters, for heaven's sake. How could Amelia keep something like this—something so *huge* and life changing—from her? And be with a man old enough to be her father!

Was Eve so removed from her sister's life that Amelia hadn't thought she would want to *know*? Want to share in the joy and anticipation of a child?

Fortunately there wasn't time for her burgeoning emotional crisis, because Alain was unbuckling her from her seat and guiding her to the exit. And before she knew it Amelia was throwing herself at Eve and clutching her close—as close as she could get with her huge belly—as if Eve was the last survivor of a nuclear holocaust.

"Oh, thank God you're safe," she whispered hoarsely in Eve's ear. "I thought…I thought… Oh, *darn*," she sobbed, giving Eve a fierce hug before moving back a few inches. Her huge blue eyes sparkled with tears as she greedily took in Eve's cleverly disguised bruises. "Look at me, bawling all over you, and you're the one who should be bawling."

She sniffed and laughed at the same time. Probably at Eve's expression. Which was most likely blank with shock…and anguish—because there was no doubt that she was hurt. Deeply hurt by her twin's secrets.

"Looks like a fiancé isn't the only thing you've been keeping from me," Eve said quietly, reaching out to brush the tears from her sister's cheeks. They'd been born only minutes apart, but she'd always felt like a much older sibling. Caring for Amelia, shielding her from their circumstances, had become a habit that was hard to break.

An indecipherable expression flashed across Amelia's face, leaving her flushed and glowing—and looking like a kid caught pilfering cookies. But she was radiant with health and contentment.

Eve closed her eyes on the rush of emotions, most of which she couldn't identify, and suddenly she felt like an outsider. No longer the most important person in her sister's life.

Unaware of Eve's emotional turmoil, Amelia gave a strangled sob. "I know—and I'm sorry, *really* sorry. It's just that…" She bit her lip and sent the man behind Eve a look filled with guilt, apprehension and stubbornness.

Eve glanced over her shoulder and caught the look of gentle reproof the pilot aimed at her twin. "You should have told her, Lia," he said. "Hitting her with everything at once isn't fair."

Amelia—*Lia?*—flashed Eve a worried look, and chewed on her thumbnail. "I know, Dad. I'm sorry. But she wouldn't have come if I'd told her."

Wait... *What?* Eve froze, her eyes darting between her sister and the pilot, widening with shocked disbelief. Her first thought was, *Thank God he's not her fiancé*, the second... *"D-Dad?"*

She shook her head, as though to clear the sudden buzzing in her ears. A buzzing that got louder the longer her head whipped between the two of them. She was giving herself whiplash, but...*what the hell?*

"What the hell do you mean... *Dad?*" she demanded, gaping at her sister as her world abruptly tilted, suddenly wavered and dipped before her eyes—even when she blinked rapidly to clear them.

"If this is a joke," she rasped, "it isn't... It's—" She lifted a hand to her fuzzy head, feeling abruptly lightheaded.

Alarmed, Alain stepped toward her, and in that instant the sun caught his eyes and she—*oh, damn*—she sucked in a wobbly breath and swayed. She really needed to sit down. Because the vague sense of familiarity she'd experienced earlier struck her again—with the force of a level-five hurricane.

Those eyes were...*hers.* Exactly like hers.

Her shocked denial emerged as a strangled gurgle and she stumbled backward...away from those reaching hands. Away from the appalling truth.

Her last thought was, *Will this nightmare never end?*

Eve opened her eyes and wondered if she was right back where she'd started, with a sexy sea god leaning over her as she lay on an old rattan sofa in the waiting room at Tiki Sea & Air.

She half expected a hoarse voice to call out a guttural, *Ia ora na e Maeva*, but then she blinked her surroundings into focus and realized that the worried sea god wasn't her sexy, grumpy pilot but a younger, sweeter version, with soft brown eyes. There was enough resemblance to have her jolting—as if her internal balance had been thrown for a crazy loop.

Pressing a shaky hand to her queasy stomach, she squeaked when tearful, *pregnant* Amelia shoved him roughly aside. Before she could utter a protesting gasp her twin had thrown herself at her and was sobbing into her neck, her huge beachball belly cutting off her air.

The younger version of Chase—*ohmigod, she'd told Chase she'd come to stop her sister from marrying a loser*—sent Eve an apologetic grimace and gently pried Amelia's death grip from around Eve's neck.

"Lia, sweetheart, you're crushing her," he murmured soothingly, and when Amelia just gave another loud sob he said more firmly, "She's starting to go blue."

With a ragged laugh Amelia abruptly let go and plopped down on the floor beside the sofa—which, Eve finally realized, wasn't old at all and was luxurious and comfortable. As was the large, airy room they were in.

Before she could take in the rest of the decor her gaze came to a screeching halt, locking on to the fourth person in the room. Alain… *Al*…Broussard. The pilot. Her…*father*?

I'm hallucinating. There must be some flower blooming around here with hallucinogenic properties, or the coffee I had this morning was spiked.

An awkward silence followed, during which everyone watched Eve staring silently at the older man as though they expected her to…what? Start yelling? Freak out? *Believe me, I'm too stunned to resort to tantrums.* But freaking out was a distinct possibility. And her head felt like it was about to explode.

Chase's brother finally rubbed his white face, looking as shaky as she felt. "I think this calls for a drink."

"I'll help," Alain murmured, and that odd yearning was back in his eyes as he gazed at Eve. Eyes so much like hers it was freaky—and too much for her to process.

Once they were alone, Eve continued to stare at the empty doorway, not wanting to deal with any more surprises. But since she couldn't escape, because she was on another island—*yay!*—she sighed and sat up, swinging her legs off the couch.

She lifted a shaky hand to her head and breathed carefully until the urge to lie down faded. Her sister was waiting not so patiently for her to say something. But...what was there to say? Okay, *fine*. She had *plenty* to say, darn it. She just didn't trust herself to voice any of it. Not until she'd recovered her brain.

And, she decided, staring down at her bare feet and wondering idly what had happened to her new sandals, not until she'd made her sister suffer just a little.

Her head was pounding and she wished almost desperately she could rewind the clock. Back to the previous night...the past three days...when she and Chase—

Her thoughts abruptly halted as the truth blindsided her like a blow to the temple. *Chase. Ohmigod.* And then humiliation—and a healthy dose of fury—filled her. He'd known. *Had* to have known about...about— Oh, yeah, she thought, catching sight of her sister's huge belly, *that*.

Of course he knew. You couldn't see Amelia and *not* know. Why hadn't he told her? Warned her? Especially after— She buried her face in her hands to hide from the memory that he hadn't said a word about anything, had let her ramble on about leaving as soon as she'd stopped her sister from marrying someone she barely knew.

She gave a silent snort. Seemed like her sister and Chase's brother knew each other pretty damn *well*.

"Are you really mad?"

Amelia's tearful voice wobbled into the thick silence, bringing Eve's whirling thoughts to a screeching halt. Slowly turning her head, she glimpsed her sister's fearful, hopeful expression through the gaps in her fingers. It was a reminder that Amelia was waiting for her to say something.

She sighed. "I came here to stop you from marrying a man you barely know," she admitted, her words scraping over a raw, tight throat. She inhaled and exhaled a few times to calm herself, before dropping her hands and looking—*really* looking—at her twin for the first time. "Only to find you pregnant, looking like you're about to pop, and already *living* with this guy you 'barely know.' And your... *father*? What the hell...?"

"*Our* father."

"You don't know that." Eve sighed, massaging her aching temples.

"I *do* know, Evie," Amelia argued gently. "All your life you've felt different because your eyes are...*weird*. Your word, not mine," she spluttered with a laugh, when Eve narrowed her "weird" eyes at her. "They were different from the rest of us and it bothered you. But when I saw Alain—Dad—I knew. Besides, what are the chances that two unrelated people have the exact same eyes—the exact same shape, the exact same color?" Without waiting for Eve to comment, Amelia continued, almost bubbling over with excitement. "And guess what else you inherited?"

"The urge to strangle you?" Eve asked dryly, not yet willing to forgive her twin.

Laughter bubbled up Amelia's throat as she hugged her and then planted a noisy kiss on Eve's knee. "No, silly." She grinned, excitement bringing back the joy that always seemed to light her up from the inside. A joy Eve would do anything to protect. "He's a doctor too. A military medic, actually. He was stationed in Hawaii, when he and Mom met. He runs the small clinic in town now."

A military medic? That *was* a surprise—and it kind of explained Eve's affinity for medicine.

"You were determined to track down your father even when I told you not to waste your time and money on all those investigators? Most of whom took your money and produced nothing but dead ends. And what for? A man who abandoned our mother when she found out she was pregnant?"

"He's *your* father too," Amelia pointed out sharply. Then, as though unable to help herself, she babbled on, looking beyond excited. "And he didn't even know she was pregnant, Evic. Mom lied. He was redeployed before she even found out. He didn't know about us."

"A likely story," Eve said wearily, shoving her hair off her face. But mentally she recalled all the other lies her mother had told—to them, to her countless men. It was just like Chloe to manipulate everyone into feeling sorry for her.

"It's true. And the best thing is we can be a family now…a *real* family. Just like we always dreamed. I can't wait till you get to know him, Evie. He's wonderful. Everyone adores him."

Eve refrained from pointing out that they'd *always* had a family—each other.

"What about your fiancé?"

"Jude?" She giggled, flushing wildly. "We met in Hawaii. He was attending some hoteliers' conference and I was singing in that hotel nightclub when he came in. It was just like Mom said. Eyes meeting across a crowded room and—*wham!* Love at first sight."

Not wanting to upset Amelia by pointing out where "love at first sight" had got her mother, Eve said, "So what are you doing here?"

"He owns it. Well Chase does but Jude does all the managing…and stuff," Amelia admitted, blithely unaware of the shock her words caused Eve.

First a seaplane and now a resort?

"So, I guess I can't talk you into going back home?"

"What? *No!*" Amelia looked horrified at the suggestion. "I love Jude more than anything. He's my soul mate. Besides, Dad's here too. We…" She placed a protective hand over her belly. "We're a family now. I'm never going back."

Eve noticed *she* hadn't been included and tried to swallow the hurt. But Amelia must have seen her expression, and with a twin's instinct she grabbed Eve's hand and squeezed.

"You know I love you, Evie. I'll always love you. You're my twin. My best friend. But I can't go back. Not even for you. But I want you to stay…and not just for the wedding." When Eve opened her mouth to remind her of her job, Amelia hastily added, "At least until after the birth. I always wanted you to be there when my baby was born. Nothing has changed."

Yet everything *had* changed, but rather than remind her twin, she sighed instead. Ignoring everything but the mention of her baby, Eve sent her sister a wry look. "You *do* know you're carrying twins, right?"

Amelia's attempt to look surprised was ruined by the secret little smile tugging at her mouth. "How can you tell?"

"Well," Eve snorted, "other than the fact that you look about twelve months pregnant?"

Amelia pouted, then burst out laughing. "Yeah…" She grinned. "Other than that."

Placing her fingers on her sister's wrist, Eve checked her pulse. "I'm a qualified OB-GYN, remember? Twins are more likely to have twins. Besides, no one can be *that* pregnant with just one infant. Unless you swallowed a beach ball?" she observed with sisterly candor.

Amelia just smiled serenely, taking Eve's hand and placing it on her baby bump. She looked happier and more content than Eve could ever remember seeing her. Clearly the island, being in love and being pregnant agreed with her.

"No beach ball," Amelia murmured dreamily. "Just two perfect little girls, lying side by side." She looked at Eve, her eyes sparkling with unshed tears. "Just like us."

Suddenly the hard belly bulged beneath Eve's hand. She identified a knee, then a foot, as the infant kicked at her hand in greeting. She couldn't prevent a misty laugh from emerging.

She was going to be an aunt.

And soon, if she read the signs correctly.

"Hi, baby," she said softly, gently massaging the restless infant until it quieted.

Eyes locked on Eve's face, Amelia sucked in a wobbly breath. "I'm scared, Evie," she admitted softly, "but I can't wait to meet them. I'm going to be the best mom, I promise."

Enormously moved by a flood of intense emotion, Eve swallowed hard and took her twin's face between her palms. They hadn't had the best role model.

She studied Amelia carefully before saying softly, "I know you are, darling." She leaned forward and kissed her twin's forehead. "Seems like you found your happily-ever-after, after all."

And you don't really need me anymore.

"Yes." Amelia sighed blissfully and placed her hands over Eve's. "And you will too, Evie, I just know it." She turned her head and kissed Eve's palm, her mischievous glance peeking from beneath her lashes. "Maybe it will be sooner than you think too. There's a local custom that says if you meet someone the moment just before the sun sinks into the sea, you're destined to be together."

Eve rolled her eyes and slid her hands free. "Right. And the tooth fairy really took our teeth when we were six."

They shared a laugh at the memory of Eve hiding her tooth until Amelia's had come out, so they could put them under their pillows together.

She sobered. She was genuinely happy for Amelia, de-

spite her misgivings. Misgivings, she admitted, that came
from their difficult childhood and their mother's death during a birth gone wrong.

Eve had learnt the hard way that things often went
wrong even with the best care. And, with just a military
medic in attendance, Eve worried that history would once
again repeat itself for Amelia. She didn't want to lose another person she loved.

"You look disgustingly healthy," she observed. "How
are you really?"

"Oh, I'm wonderful." Amelia beamed. "Now that you're
here, everything's perfect."

One evening a week later Eve murmured her excuses and
rose from the dinner table. She needed to escape. All the
loving looks between Amelia and Jude, the talk of babies,
weddings and family, were giving her a headache.

Or that was what she told herself. The truth was harder
to swallow. She was jealous—and ashamed of it. Although
why she should be envious of her sister's happiness, Eve
didn't know. Protecting Amelia had always been her first
priority and nothing had changed. She was so darn grateful her twin had found the stability she'd always craved.

Besides, she had her entire future ahead of her. She'd
finally accessed her messages and heard that she'd been
offered the OB-GYN fellowship in Washington. Exactly
what she'd worked so hard for, for so long.

So why hadn't she accepted? Why had she said she
needed a few days to think it over? And why did the
thought of returning leave her feeling depressed?

It was everything she'd ever wanted.

Wasn't it?

Of course it was, she told herself firmly, changing direction and heading for the beach instead of the veranda
as she'd initially planned. She needed to be alone to sort
through the wild pendulum swings of emotion that had her

happy and excited one minute, filled with dread the next and then feeling a yawning emptiness a minute after that.

If she didn't know better she would think she was pregnant. She wasn't, and it frankly irritated her to think that her plans were coming together and all she could think about was—

Yeah. Dumb, dumb, dumb.

Sighing, she brought her mind back from straying in dangerous directions and kicked off her sandals, pausing a moment to enjoy the warm silky sand beneath her feet before wading into the shallows. Cool, crystal-clear water instantly rushed over her feet as though eager to welcome her.

Over the past week she'd been frustratingly unsuccessful in not thinking about Chase. She'd even dreamed about him. Several times. So often, in fact, that she'd started thinking there must be something in the air that had drugged her with a lust spell.

She'd kept herself busy taking care of her sister and spending a few hours each day with Alain—*she still couldn't think of him as her father*—at the small clinic. It had been…*nice.* The clinic more than her father, although she was getting to know him and had to admit she was glad her sister had tracked him down.

And yet despite the circumstances—or maybe because of them, she admitted wryly—she felt utterly alone.

She sighed. It was time to go home. Back to her life, her work. Where she wouldn't have time to obsess about things she couldn't change and wasn't certain she would even if she could.

Wrapping her arms around herself, she stared at the giant fiery ball hovering lazily on the far horizon and came to a difficult decision. She would accept the Washington position tonight because, as beautiful and tranquil as the island was, her sister no longer needed her. And since that was the case… Well, there was nothing keeping her here.

Nothing at all.

CHAPTER TWELVE

At the sight of the lone figure standing motionless at the water's edge, Chase came to an abrupt stop. A gauzy calf-length dress billowed around the lithe feminine form, teased by the gentle evening breeze. He knew instinctively who it was. His body had recognized her long before his brain caught up.

Eve.

Shoving his hands in the pockets of his ratty jeans, he looked his fill. The deepening glow of the setting sun highlighted the curvy body beneath the gossamer fabric. Even as his heart pounded and his body stirred, the unbearable loneliness surrounding her made his chest ache.

He exhaled in a long, silent curse. *Damn*. He didn't want to feel this way. Although exactly what he *did* feel wasn't clear. He knew only that the sight of her made him want to tackle her down onto the sand and have his merry way with her. One night hadn't been nearly enough to get her out of his system. But, after the way he'd left, she'd probably knee him in the nuts if he so much as looked sideways at her.

He snorted. Big deal. So he was a mess. He would just become *un*messed. He'd done it before.

But then again… He'd been so sure that when he saw her again all the conflicting emotions he'd practically fallen over himself to escape would turn out to be nothing more than lust for a beautiful woman. Oh, yeah—and the memory of spectacular sex.

Because the sex *had* been spectacular, he admitted. One-of-a-kind spectacular. The kind you waited your entire life to experience. The kind you wanted to keep having until the raging urgency cooled. Or until someone left. Because she *would* leave—and soon, if what his brother said was true. She'd received that offer from some fancy DC medical facility and would leave as soon as her new passport arrived.

Or sooner if she really wanted.

He'd returned to the crash site and found her laptop and purse. Instead of forwarding them he'd taken them back to Port Laurent without saying a word to anyone.

He didn't have a specific reason for keeping it to himself—at least none that made sense. One thing he *did* know was that having her hadn't cooled his jets. It had just made the ache deeper, the need sharper. It had also made him question the strange restlessness he'd been experiencing lately.

And now that he was standing here, witnessing the stark loneliness surrounding her, he saw the restlessness for what it was.

It was loneliness.

He was lonely. And it was all her fault.

He'd been sane and happy, bouncing around the South Pacific in his plane, free as a bird and doing exactly what pleased him. It had taken surviving an air crash with a mouthy, stressed-out doctor with soft ivory skin and amber-gold eyes for him to realize what he was missing.

He was missing…*connection*. Yeah, that was what it was. A connection with someone other than family. A personal and intimate connection.

And if he thought he could find it anywhere else he'd leave a vapor trail across the South Pacific.

Yet here he was, heart pounding, palms sweating, because he had feelings for a woman who couldn't wait to leave her own vapor trail. Feelings that left him unable to sleep, tied up in so many knots his sanity had begun to unravel—one *get real* look, one *you're an idiot* smile, one feminine snort and an eye roll at a time.

If he didn't know any better he would say... He would think he was in l—

Wait...*what*? He sucked in a shocked breath and slapped a hand over where his heart had stopped in his chest. *Love?* He staggered and thrust out the hand not clutching his chest, grabbed hold of the closest tree.

Could he be in...? *No way! No freaking way.* He was just having a coronary. Yep, that was what it was. He was just... *Oh, man.*

He gaped at the woman responsible for his mental melt-down and the truth hit him with all the subtlety of a sledge-hammer.

Well, hell. Wasn't that just great? he thought on a surge of resentment. He was in freaking love with a woman so wrong for him she might have been from another planet. And when a little voice in his head snickered—*Look at Mr. I'm-too-cool-to-fall-for-that-again...cut off at the knees by the woman least likely to stick around*—he sagged against the tree, knees wobbly, blood roaring through his head.

No wonder... No damn wonder he felt like he was los-ing his grip, he thought on a fresh surge of resentment. He'd lost his head along with his heart—to a woman who couldn't wait to be thousands of miles away. But there was no doubt—no doubt at all—that he was... He was— His breath whooshed out. He was in...*love*?

Breathing heavily, he glared at Eve, standing in para-dise as though she *hadn't* stolen his heart along with his mind. And before he knew it his feet were taking him to-ward her, as though obeying some command that certainly hadn't come from his brain.

But now that he was moving he'd just go down there and give her a piece of his mind, he thought furiously. How dared she make him crazy? Who did she think she was, coming here to paradise and messing with his carefree life?

She stiffened the instant he came up beside her, clearly seething with her own jumble of conflicting emotions and thoughts.

"Go away," she said, turning away as though she couldn't bear to look at him. That stung, but he figured he deserved it for sneaking out like he had, so he let it go. What he couldn't let go was her—not without a fight.

"This is your fault, you know," he growled when she began to move away.

Her purposeful stride halted and after a couple beats she turned, her face shadowed by the approaching night. But Chase knew she was staring at him as though he'd lost his mind.

"My fault? *My fault?*" Her voice rose with disbelief, interrupting his mental litany of the things she was guilty of. Now that she was looking right at him he noticed the anger glinting in her golden-brown eyes.

That surprised him—okay, only surprised him a little—because she'd been the one to put a moratorium on their... on sex. But then she was a woman. He should have known she would change her mind. *Had* she changed her mind?

"You said one night only," he pointed out, sounding like a petulant kid. "I was just giving you what you wanted."

"You don't know what I want, Mr. Gallagher. How could you? You didn't stick around long enough to find out."

Yeah, well, he hadn't wanted to get kicked in the teeth either. But he couldn't very well say that, so he racked his brain for something to say and finally came up with, "I hear you're spending time with your father?"

The instant the words emerged he knew it was the wrong thing to say.

Her head whipped around and in the gathering darkness he saw her jaw clench and her eyes narrow. "Really?" she drawled coolly. "We're going to talk about *this*? About my *father*? A man you knew about but didn't see fit to mention? Or how about the fact that your brother got my sister pregnant—with twins?"

In the half-light their eyes met and held. A primal awareness snaked down his spine and he opened his mouth to say... He didn't have a freaking clue. Because all he could think about was grabbing her and kissing the hell out of her.

When he remained silent she sighed and her shoulders sagged. Almost immediately they straightened again—that backbone of steel he admired, stiffening her resolve.

"You know what? Never mind. It doesn't matter because I'm leaving."

His gut clenched. "Leaving?"

"Tomorrow. Maybe the day after."

Without waiting for his response she turned and walked away. Instinctively he reached out and caught her hand, wrapping his fingers around her delicate wrist.

"Just like that?" he demanded, feeling her pulse jitter beneath his touch. "You'd leave your sister? Your twin and her babies? They're your *nieces*, for God's sake. And what about your father? What about—?"

She yanked at her arm and rounded on him, her eyes spitting angry fire, her body vibrating with barely leashed fury.

"What *about* him?" she demanded, her voice tight with an emotion that went way beyond anger. "He's a stranger—a man I never knew existed until a week ago. A man who didn't give a damn about the woman he'd knocked up even enough to leave a forwarding address."

She sucked in a couple shaky breaths before continuing, her voice low and raw.

"I had to take care of them. *All* of them. My mother, my sister and then my grandmother. Because beautiful, talented and vivacious Chloe was too busy looking for the next exciting man, the next dream job, the next adventure. She didn't care that her children were hungry and wearing clothes rejected by welfare. Or that her mother was too sick to manage two jobs as well as two little kids." Her breath hitched. "Was he there to protect us when my mother's men sneaked into our bedroom at night?"

Shocked to his soul, Chase could only stare at her while her ragged breathing tore at something deep inside. "Did they…? Did you…?" He couldn't voice the awful, terrible things he was thinking.

"No," Eve said, so quietly that he had to strain to hear her above the quiet *shush-shush* of the waves that lapped at their feet. "But not for want of trying. I fought and screamed bloody blue murder until my mother roused herself enough to kick him out. And then I learnt to defend myself—and Amelia. It didn't stop, of course, but our neighbor, Mrs. Friedman, was a kind old lady. When things got bad she'd let Amelia and me sneak in through the fire escape."

"Eve—"

"It doesn't matter," Eve said wearily. "Not anymore. I vowed to make something of myself and I have. Besides, Amelia doesn't need me anymore. She has her happily-ever-after. She has Jude and the babies." Her voice hitched again and she gestured to the island. "She finally has the home, the family, she always wanted."

Chase caught sight of the glitter in her eyes and his throat ached. He clenched his jaw against the urge to wrap her close and promise she'd never be alone. Because hearing about what she'd had to go through, the strength and courage of a little girl determined to protect her twin… God, how could he *not* love her? How could he not want to offer her anything she wanted…everything she deserved?

"And you, Eve?" he demanded quietly. "What do *you* want?"

After a short pause she turned away, and a soft, "Nothing…" came to him on the warm breeze.

Before he could blurt out all the dumb things whirling

around in his head he heard a shout. They turned as one as Jude came tearing down the beach.

"Eve!" Jude gasped, looking white and wild-eyed. "Come quickly. It's…it's Lia."

CHAPTER THIRTEEN

HEART LURCHING INTO her throat, Eve lifted her dress above her knees and took off up the beach toward the house. Her sister had looked tired and pale all day, and despite her protestations that she was fine Eve had made her rest. Her blood pressure, which had been a little high, had come right back down after her rest, but she'd complained of a nagging backache.

She was almost thirty-four weeks pregnant—about the time most twin births occurred—and lower back pain was normal. It was also right about the time in her second pregnancy that their mother had died. And although her mother hadn't had the kind of care Jude had insisted on for Amelia, things—bad things—could still happen.

Jude had spared no expense in having a high-tech nursery-cum-birthing-room installed, along with two incubators, oxygen tanks and a fully equipped emergency trauma kit. Just in case.

Clearly Jude could afford to pamper his family.

With the brothers on her heels, Eve tore across the grass and up the stairs, bursting into the house with a frantic, "Amelia, where are you?"

"We're in here," their father called frantically from the family room, just as a scream tore through the silence.

Eve changed direction, surging into the room to find him kneeling beside the hunched figure of her twin. The dark stain surrounding her confirmed Eve's worst fears. Amelia's water had broken.

"What happened?"

"She got up from the table and…and suddenly clutched her belly." Jude gulped at her shoulder, looking pale and shaky.

Alain was pale too, and she noted the faintest tremble in the hand he used to smooth back her sister's hair. He'd probably spent his entire military career caring for men, and didn't know a thing about birthing premature twins. Besides, when it was someone you cared about stress levels rose up the wazoo.

"Jude, help me get Amelia to the nursery," she ordered briskly, dropping to her haunches beside her sister to check her pulse. "Chase, go to the nursery, plug in the incubators and get the sterile units ready. I'll also need an old clean T-shirt and a pair of shorts. Dad, prep the emergency tactical kit. We might need it."

For a couple of beats everyone froze, including Amelia, who was hunched over, clutching her belly. They all stared at Eve as though she'd grown horns and spikes down the length of her back.

She frowned at their stunned expressions. "What?" she demanded. "Am I going too fast? Fine, I'll talk slower. Jude, help—"

"No," Amelia panted, grabbing Eve's hand in a painful grip that became crushing as the contraction reached its peak. "You…you…called…him…Dad."

Eve frowned, concern for her sister uppermost in her mind. Especially as Amelia's pulse was racing—a sure sign that something was wrong.

"Who?" she asked absently as Alain and Chase disappeared.

"Da-a-ad!" Amelia wailed as another contraction seized her. "You…you called him Dad."

"Don't be ridiculous," she denied absently, looking to her brother-in-law-to-be. "Jude. *Now!*"

Jude jumped at the order, seeming to come out of his trance. Within seconds he and Eve had Amelia up, practically carrying her out the living room.

"Don't touch anything until you've all scrubbed up," she ordered on entering the nursery. She helped Amelia onto her side. "Draw your legs up to your belly, sweetie. It'll be more comfortable while I get suited up, and you won't be tempted to push." She looked at Jude, who was standing there as though someone had hit him in the head. "Don't leave her. She's going to be focused on the pain, so you'll have to breathe with her."

He sucked in a shaky breath, looking around wildly. "I...uh...I don't think I can do this."

She stepped forward just as Amelia gave another hair-raising wail and squeezed his arm. "You can," she said in a low, firm tone, her gaze holding his until his eyes cleared. "It's going to get a little rough on her and she's going to need you to be strong. Besides, I'm here. Doing all the easy stuff."

After a short pause he sucked in a deep breath and nodded. "All right. Where...um...do you want me?"

"Just help her breathe. I'm going to wash up."

Without waiting for him to obey, Eve turned away and stripped out of the dress she was wearing, reaching for the shorts and T-shirt Chase handed over.

It was clear from the size of them that he'd raided his brother's wardrobe, but she didn't have time to find anything that fitted. Besides, he was looking a little stunned. Kind of like when she'd blurted out all her old childhood issues. Issues she would have sworn she'd been over for a long time.

Clearly she wasn't.

But she didn't have time to revisit her childhood, she mused, rushing over to the basin to scrub up. It was over and done and she wasn't that vulnerable, scared little kid anymore. She was a medical professional, about to deliver premature twins.

Her sister's babies.

The thought jolted her, but she firmed her jaw, turning and shrugging into the sterile gown her father held ready. By the time she was suited up Chase was edging out the door, looking alarmed and like he was wishing he was a thousand miles away.

But he wasn't. He'd chosen tonight to reappear, after eight days of silence, so he might as well be useful.

"I'm going to need you," she said, locking gazes with him and brushing aside her embarrassment at her earlier outburst.

His mouth dropped open. "I...uh...*wha-a-t?*"

"All hands on deck," she insisted briskly, trying not to smile at his hunted expression.

He swallowed. "What about Jude and...and Al?"

"They'll soon be pretty busy and won't be able to help this end."

He paled. "This...? Oh, no. No way in hell I can do... *that.*"

Eve sighed and did a mental eye roll. "Do you fix your own planes?"

Surprise and confusion crossed his face. "What does that have to do with anything?"

"Think of it as fixing an engine."

He gaped at her. "You're joking, right? I can handle grease. I just can't handle bloo— *Holy hell!*" He shoved shaking hands through his hair, looking a little wild-eyed. "Why is she screaming like that? Is she dying?"

"No, she isn't." Eve reached for the pressure cuff. "Jude, bring Amelia to the edge of the bed and get behind her. She'll need you to support her shoulders," she ordered, dropping to her knees at the bottom of the bed, where Alain had already placed a sheet of plastic. "Don't let her lie flat. Dad, where's the fetal monitor?"

She turned back to find Chase still hovering in the doorway.

Her gaze caught and held his. "Can I count on you?"

His eyes darkened to a mysterious stormy gray, their depths swirling with intensity. After a weighty pause, he nodded. "Always."

For some odd reason a shiver worked its way up Eve's spine. She held his gaze for another beat before nodding. "Good," she rasped, her throat strangely tight, before abruptly turning away—because now wasn't the time to think about its significance. "Then bring that chux pad and help me get it under her."

By the time Alain had fitted the fetal monitor, the pressure cuff was inflated and beeping out its reading. It was a little high, she noted, but not dangerously so.

Amelia suddenly sucked in a sharp breath and Eve saw her body arch as a powerful contraction gripped her. "Breathe through it," she advised calmly. "Breathe, sweetie, but try not to push."

Amelia cried out and grabbed a fistful of Jude's shirt.

"I...need...to push!" she yelled, panting.

"Not yet," Eve said firmly, looking up into her sister's wild eyes between her propped knees. "I see a baby's shoulder and I'm going to have to reposition her."

Amelia gave another long wail that would have raised the hair on her neck if Eve hadn't been used to the sounds of labor. Amelia grabbed both Jude's forearms and Eve caught his pained grimace as Amelia squeezed until her knuckles whitened. The man was likely to have bruises later.

"Jude," Eve said, catching his attention. "I need you to keep her calm while I move the baby." She waited until his glassy eyes cleared. "Can you do that?"

He looked shell-shocked. "Uh...yeah...sure. Calm... got it."

Amelia started sobbing, her words an almost incoherent wail as she kept saying over and over that she couldn't do it, that she'd changed her mind.

She sounded so terrified that Eve reached up to squeeze her knee. "You can do this, sweetie. Just relax for a minute while I reposition her. After that she'll slide right out, okay?" She looked at her father, who was frowning at the fetal monitor. "Alain...Dad?"

He turned his head and Eve could see the fear and concern he was trying to hide. Without changing her expression she quickly noted that one baby's heart rate was rising, way above one-forty.

"Can you feel for the baby's other shoulder and bottom while I work on easing her around?"

"Piece of cake," he said, placing his large, capable hands on her sister's hard belly.

It wasn't a piece of cake, but Eve was grateful for his cheerfulness, knowing it would calm her sister.

"Eve, what's happening? Is everything all right?" Jude demanded, his voice a little higher than normal. He was sweating, and his breathing was almost as ragged as Amelia's. The hand he lifted to smooth Amelia's hair off her damp face was unsteady.

"Everything's fine," she assured him, with a calmness she told herself was real. "Just keep doing what you're doing. And for God's sake, Amelia, don't push until I tell you to."

Amelia made a growling sound in the back of her throat that Eve might have found amusing at any other time. She gently inserted two fingers beneath the baby's left shoulder and carefully pushed until it disappeared. Then she felt around until she'd identified the back of the neck and the head, supporting both as she cautiously eased the infant into a better position. Within seconds the head appeared.

"Thank God." She huffed out her relief, soothing her sister as another contraction gripped her. "You're doing great," she soothed quietly. "Not long now and you can push."

When Amelia screamed and arched her back Jude leaned forward, fisting a hand in Eve's T-shirt. He yanked her upwards. "It's killing her! *Do* something!"

Without a beat she shrugged him off, her attention on the sight of the head emerging. "Get it together, Jude," she ordered quietly. "She needs to know she can count on you."

"She can… She does… Oh, God. We're not doing *this* again." He grabbed Eve again and shook her. "Do you hear me? We…are…*not*…doing…this…again!"

"Hey, bro…" Chase suddenly appeared beside her. He pried Jude's fingers off her. "They heard you in Honolulu. Chill. Get a grip, man. Eve knows what she's doing. Let her do it."

She sent Chase a quick look of gratitude, faintly amused by his fierceness. "It's okay," she murmured, transferring her attention to Jude. He was a wreck, so she smiled encouragingly at him. "Fathers tend to get a little intense. It's allowed."

Helpless tears swam in his soft brown eyes and for a moment hers got a little misty too.

She inhaled. "We're doing this now," she said, transferring her gaze to her sister's sweat-slicked face. "Amelia. You can push on the next contr— Oh, yes. Just like that. Another one. Nearly there…"

The baby's head suddenly cleared, face downward, one shoulder still wedged tight. She gently supported the tiny head and neck.

"Breathe through the next one for just a sec…" When the tension lessened, she eased the left shoulder free. "That's great," she murmured, and took the heated towel her father handed her. "Just one more push and you'll be holding your baby. What are we calling her?"

"Is—Isabella," Amelia gasped.

The rest of the infant slid out into her waiting hands.

"I've got her," she said in triumph, her gaze flying up to connect with her twin's for a second. "Isabella. And she's beautiful."

The baby gave a muffled squawk, then let out a lusty cry, her little fists waving at the indignity she had just experienced. Eve gave a wobbly laugh as a collective sigh of relief followed. With her sister laughing and crying, and panting with exertion, Eve dried the baby as Alain applied a plastic clip to the umbilical cord and then cut it.

She swopped the wet towel for the dry one that Chase held out. Their eyes connected for an instant. She froze, and the room and its occupants went *whoosh*, leaving just the two of them floating in a vacuum. The only thing keeping her from drifting away was the invisible link between their locked gazes.

Ears buzzing, heart pounding, Eve felt a tingle skate across her skin. As though something profound and earth-shattering had just occurred. And then for one blinding instant her mind cleared—and she staggered.

Oh, God. She'd gone and done the unthinkable. She'd committed emotional suicide.

She shook her head to clear the unwelcome thought, but the truth remained—a neon light blazing in the darkness.

She gone and fallen for a sexy, grumpy flyboy with commitment issues. But that wasn't just ridiculous…it was impossible. No one could fall in love in less than a fortnight—well, three days, actually.

It was… It was… She blinked rapidly to clear her vision. *Dammit.* It was truc. This…this madness could only mean one thing.

She was in love with Chase Gallagher.

He must have seen something in her face, because he stepped forward, his gaze filled with concern.

That "something" might very well have been horror… and panic…because not only did he not love her back, he'd *bought* a plane to get the hell away from her.

* * *

Chase's heart leaped into his throat. One minute Eve had been staring at him as though he was the only person in the room, the next her expression had turned stunned—as though something earth-shattering had just occurred to her.

And by look on her face it had filled her with horror.

He reached out, catching her shoulders as she stumbled back a step. Was there something wrong with her? With the baby? Or was it Amelia?

His eyes flashed to his brother's fiancée and he saw she was moaning again, her back arched off the bed. She was also chanting.

"Oh, God, oh, God, make it stop."

He shook Eve and she abruptly came out of her trance.

"What's wrong?" she demanded, instinctively cradling the now quiet infant.

"I was about to ask you the same thing—" he began, but she wasn't listening, swinging around as Alain interrupted quietly.

"Uh…Evelyn, darling, I think we have a problem.'

"Here," she said, thrusting the tiny bundle at Chase.

His arms automatically closed around the baby, but he was shocked speechless that she would trust him with a fragile newborn.

Heart pounding, knees knocking, Chase stared down at the tiny face with its big eyes, cute little nose and rosebud mouth. What the hell was he supposed to do with a fragile scrap of life that weighed as much as a kitten? Didn't Eve know that he'd never held a baby in his life? What if he dropped her? What if he—?

"Keep her warm," she ordered. "And keep an eye on her breathing and her color."

"But…"

"She needs to stay nice and pink."

"Wait!" he said a little frantically. "I—"

"Busy here, Chase," she said impatiently, already focus-ing on the problem.

Chase noticed immediately that there was blood. *Oh, man.* He gulped when Amelia arched her back again and gave the kind of scream that sounded like fingernails scrap-ing down a chalkboard. It echoed in his head as his eyes were drawn to the blood... He blinked and felt his world tilt. A lot of blood.

"Man up," she snapped, taking in his abrupt loss of color. "Isabella needs you. *I* need you."

Without waiting for him to respond—and he couldn't anyway...not with his stomach sitting in his throat—Eve turned away, issuing orders in a quiet, firm voice.

He stumbled backward until his shoulder hit the wall. Through the buzzing in his ears he heard her say some-thing that sounded like placental abruption. Then she began ordering Al around in a way that calmed him even as his stress levels rose through the freaking roof.

Something was wrong.

He didn't want to know what his brother was going through, but he knew that whatever it was, it was bad. Al-most blindly, he gazed down at the tiny girl in his arms. "If your guardian angel is close, kid, I think you'd better start praying. You gotta be strong, sweet Belle. Your mama needs you. Your sister needs you."

She blinked up at him and for an instant he thought that maybe she'd understood him, because her little fore-head creased, her eyes locked on his. But that was impos-sible. Babies couldn't see clearly. At least that was what he'd heard.

Everything happened really quickly then. And despite his squeamish stomach, Chase couldn't keep his eyes off Eve, off the way she handled the crisis—calmly, clearly the one in charge.

Alain administered an injection almost directly into Amelia's stomach that had Chase's own giving a greasy roll. As he watched, Eve prepped Amelia's belly with a swab of some brownish fluid. And then—*oh, man...* His head spun. He was going to pass right out, and then they'd have two crises on their hands. He sucked in a steadying breath and cradled the baby closer, as though to protect her from what was happening a short distance away.

Eve probed the distended belly and with one careful line of the scalpel opened Amelia up. He saw blood welling through the new incision and Amelia's cries echoed through the buzzing in his head. Before he could bellow at Eve to stop before she injured the baby, Eve's hands had slipped in—*oh, God*—and then...and then... He blinked... *Oh, wow. Look at that!* She gently eased the tiny head out, still covered with a membrane.

With a few deft moves Eve ruptured the membrane, accepted the suction thingy Alain held out and she cleared the baby's nose and mouth. Then she was lifting the tiny little body out into the world.

He was stunned and awed by what had taken less than a minute.

"Go," Alain said, quickly wrapping the baby in a towel as Eve applied a clip and severed the umbilical cord. "I'll deal with things here. Get that baby with us. Her twin needs her."

It was then that Chase realized the little body had been limp and mottled before being bundled up. His heart lurched in his chest as his eyes followed Eve's progress across the room. He felt like the room was pressing in on him as she placed the baby on a soft warmer, her body shielding the rest of the room from what she was doing.

For long tense minutes he waited, holding his breath. And just when he thought the little girl in his arms, scarcely an hour old, was going to experience a devastating loss, a thin wail broke the tense silence.

His legs gave way then, and the next minute he realized

he was sitting on the floor, staring at his niece and blinking back tears of joy and relief.

"Thank God," he murmured, dropping a gentle kiss on the baby's soft head and murmuring a word of thanks. "Those prayers worked, kiddo. She's okay. Your sister's okay. And your Aunt Eve—she's the best. She's made sure your little sister's gonna be just fine." He lifted his head, addressing his next words to Eve. "She's going to be okay, isn't she?"

Eve turned to him, her smile a bit wobbly. Her golden eyes shone with joy and love and a wild, deep relief. She blinked back tears and gave a watery laugh. "She's going to be just fine."

In that moment Chase realized she was everything he'd ever wanted. If only—

Hell, no. He was going to make her listen, keep her here. Even if he had to steal her new passport too.

CHAPTER FOURTEEN

EVE PLACED A pink and squalling Anastasia on Amelia's chest and bent down to kiss her cheek. Her twin looked up then, and in a brief telling moment all their love and shared history passed between them.

"Congratulations, Mom. You did great."

"Oh, my gosh—she's beautiful," Amelia said, looking exhausted but elated. "Where's her sister? I want to hold them both."

"She's right here," Chase said, stepping close to the bed.

In Eve's opinion he appeared a little reluctant to relinquish his precious armful. She thought back to earlier, when he'd looked like she'd handed him a box full of live grenades. Now he was wearing an expression of such stunned love, awe and heartbreak that she instinctively reached out to him.

Realizing what she was doing, she dropped her hand and turned away. She didn't need to burden him with her feelings, she thought. Besides, this was about Amelia and Jude—not her.

Alain, finishing the wound closure, looked up at that moment. He must have caught her staring at Chase, because he said quietly, "You're in love with him."

Her head whipped up, an automatic denial on her lips. "No, I—"

But Alain was gazing at her with his own brand of love and heartbreak, and her heart squeezed again.

"It doesn't matter," she murmured. "I'm leaving soon. Besides, he doesn't love me back."

"Are you so sure of that, Evie?" he asked gently, reaching out to touch an unsteady hand to her shoulder. "Are you so afraid you're unlovable?" He shook his head. "You're not, sweetheart. You just have to let people in—let them love you."

Instead of replying she just shook her head, suddenly eager to be alone. *Did* she think she was unlovable? *Did* she shut people out because of her past?

"Go meet your granddaughters, Dad. But only for a few minutes. They need to go into the incubators for a while. Especially the little one."

For a long moment he seemed conflicted, and Eve thought he meant to push her. His gaze searched hers, then he nodded and turned away—but not before he murmured, "We need to talk, Evelyn, and soon."

Eager to escape the emotionally charged moment, Eve swallowed the lump in her throat and moved off to tidy up, clearing away the debris so the new family could bond in a fresh, clean environment. Thankfully her part of the drama was over, she thought, gathering up the soiled linen and towels before quietly slipping out of the room.

At the door she looked back and drew in a long, shuddery breath as the scene hit her like a sharp blow to the heart. Her head swam and her knees buckled as something she'd been ignoring struck her with a sudden blinding clarity.

Everything that meant anything to her was right there in that room. Her twin and the man she had chosen to love, their new twin daughters, her father and—

Yes, and Chase too. Because she loved him. More than she would have thought possible. But the question was...

could she make herself vulnerable to him? Could she trust
that he wouldn't leave her?

She honestly didn't know. And the knowledge had her
taking that step away, even as her brain greedily stored
away the image of him sharing in the joy of new life. It
was one of those moments that would be seared into her
memory for all time. A moment that, if a person was open
to it, redefined their life.

It was a moment of new life, new beginnings and second chances. Because everyone deserved a second chance,
didn't they? Even her father. Because he *was* her father.
She knew that—just as she knew she'd been unfair earlier.

He wasn't to blame. Just as Chase wasn't to blame for
her fear of rejection when all he'd done was what she'd said
she wanted. A one-off thing. Nothing more.

But, knowing what she did now, how could she leave all
this behind? How could she walk away from everything
she'd always thought only her sister yearned for?

A family.

Her eyes locked unerringly on Chase and her heart
clenched. The big question she should be asking herself
was how could she stay, knowing he didn't…couldn't…
love her back?

Pressing an unsteady hand to the ache filling the center
of her chest, Eve quietly left the room. She needed a minute to herself. A minute to shore up the wall around her
heart. Because, despite what she so desperately yearned
for, it wasn't to be.

And maybe it never had been.

Chase found her in the same spot, the same pose as before.
It was like déjà vu. Only this time, instead of the glowing
sun, a huge moon illuminated the small private beach, gild-
ing the sand, the water and the woman in glowing silver.

For a moment it staggered him, had him sucking in a
sharp breath at the depth of his feelings for her. The woman

of his dreams, the woman of his heart, stood apart—isolated and alone.

"Why are you out here?" he asked quietly as he came up beside her. "They need you."

She jolted, as though he'd surprised her, and turned away, murmuring something that sounded like, "No. They don't. Not anymore."

He opened his mouth and caught a flash of something sparkling on her cheek, her lashes.

Tears?

"You're crying?"

She gave a husky laugh that reached out and grabbed him by the throat.

"Don't b-be ridiculous. What's there to cry about?"

He took her shoulders, turned her toward him. "That's what I'd like to know," he murmured, reaching up to catch another tear, sparkling like a tiny diamond on her thick lashes.

She irritably brushed his hand away, wrapping her arms protectively around her body as she put a little distance between them. Was she protecting herself from her emotions…or him?

"It…it got a bit tense there for a minute," she admitted on a ragged sigh, rubbing her upper arms briskly. "I thought we might lose her."

"Hey," he said gently, moving close, careful not to touch her. Especially as she vibrated with enough tension that he was afraid one wrong move would shatter her fragile control. "You were awesome. Amazingly calm when everyone else was panicking." He sucked in an unsteady breath at the memory. "Although I have to admit it totally grossed me out, and if I hadn't been holding Belle I most probably would have hit the floor horizontally."

Eve gave a watery laugh and then, in a move that surprised the hell out of him, she dropped her forehead onto his chest and sobbed as if her heart was breaking.

For an instant he panicked. Had he said the wrong thing?
Aw, man...

"Hey...hey," he crooned, instinctively wrapping his arms around her, pulling her in, tucking her head beneath his chin. He felt as if he was finally home—that *she* was home. Right where she belonged.

So he held her, let her cry. Knowing he could do nothing else.

A minute stretched to two, but he was in no hurry to let her go. He'd walked away once, but he wouldn't let her scare him off now. Not again. Besides, he had to show her somehow that she could count on him. Always.

"Eve... Eve... Eve..." he murmured softly, dropping a soft kiss on her head. "It's okay—everything's fine. The babies are fine. Amelia is glowing. And you'd swear that Jude—he's standing there smiling like an idiot, like he did it all himself. But you know what, babe? They need you there, celebrating with them—not out here, crying like your heart is breaking."

She stiffened, and then in an abrupt move shoved him away. He caught her wrist as she turned.

"Don't go," he urged, and his own heart squeezed in his chest, because he had a bad feeling she was gearing up to walk away. He'd seen her expression when she'd left the room and he knew, just *knew*, she was leaving.

"Why?" she asked quietly, her voice emotionless, her eyes dark and remote.

Chase's mind went abruptly blank.

"I...I..."

Misinterpreting his hesitation, Eve tried to break free, but Chase tightened his grip. He wasn't letting go. Not until he'd—

"Because...they...they need you, Eve. Amelia...the girls...your father."

There was a buzzing sound in his head and his panic ratcheted up a couple million notches when he saw the expressions chasing each other across her face. Anguish, desolation, grief. And then…right there…that backbone of steel, straightening with pride. He could feel her slipping away.

"And I…I n-n…" His throat closed but he forced the words out before he blinked and she disappeared. "I need… I need…" He took a couple ragged breaths and ended with, "I-need-you-too," in a breathless rush.

For long, tense moments Eve's gaze remained steady on his, then a quiet "Why?" drifted across the couple of feet that separated them.

He blinked. "Why?"

"Yes. Why?" Her voice was curiously emotionless. "Why should I stay when everything I've worked for is in DC?"

Panic moved through him like an oily snake, slithering and burrowing deep. "Because…because everything you care about is here. Isn't it? Besides…" He shrugged. "I need you."

For long moments she simply stared at him, until finally she blinked and turned away, hurt battling with the desperate hope in her eyes.

"I can't," she said, drawing into herself, away from him.

Chase's heart sank as she slid free from his hold. Feeling his own hands shake, he shoved them in his pockets.

"You can't?" he muttered, swallowing the last of his hope. And with it came a rising anger. Here he was, offering her everything, and all she could say was, *I can't.* "What the hell does that even *mean*?" he demanded. "You can't *what*? Stay? Love me? Need me? *What*? What the hell can't you do, Eve?"

She turned on him then, her eyes flashing with anger and a deep, deep fear. "It's not enough." And then, more quietly. "It's not enough."

"Not…*enough*?" His jaw clenched. "I offer you everything and it's…not enough?"

Her body stilled in the process of turning away. Her eyes were dark and unreadable. "What do you mean by *everything*, Chase? How can you say that and then leave?"

"Who says I'm leaving?"

"You *did* leave," Eve pointed out in a sharp reminder, and when he arched his brow she snapped, "Oh, don't look at me like that. You even bought an aircraft so you could escape." Eve was gratified to see him wince. "Really? Who *does* that?"

"An idiot," Chase muttered, and when she gave a strangled laugh, he lost his battle with his temper. He grabbed her, shook her. "An idiot in love—that's who. Why the hell do you think I didn't tell you about your passport? Why the hell do you think—?"

He stopped abruptly when he realized what he'd admitted. He let her go and shoved his hands through his hair, wondering if he could go back a couple of minutes. To when he hadn't shoved a foot in his mouth.

She blinked rapidly looking stunned. "You... My... what?"

He sighed. "Yeah. I found it," he admitted quietly. "I found it and I kept it."

Her eyes widened. "What...? Why?"

Chase turned away with an awkward laugh. "Hell, I don't know." Then he sighed and swung back, his resolve hardening. When had he become such a coward? *When you fell in love—that's when.* "Yes, I do," he countered harshly. "I was married before, did I tell you that? No?" He gave a harsh laugh. "Yeah, well I was. And it was a huge mistake. From the beginning. I promised myself I would never let a woman hurt me the way she did, and I haven't. Until you.

"It was easy to walk away from Lauren because looking back I never really loved her, not like..." He drew air into his lungs and shoved unsteady hands through his hair. "The truth is I kept your passport because I didn't want you to leave. I kept it because…because… Dammit, I didn't know it then, but I love you."

"What—what did you say?"

"I couldn't just let you walk away—" he began, but she reached up and covered his mouth with trembling fingers.

"Not that…" She gulped. "Before."

"What?" he demanded around her fingers. "That I love—?" He stopped when disbelief and desperate hope battled with the automatic denial in her eyes. "Yeah." He smiled, tension easing in his chest, his shoulders. "Yeah, I do. I love you, Eve, although I don't know why. You're uptight and mouthy and you don't know how to relax. You like to argue…"

He gave a soft laugh when her eyes narrowed. He covered her hand with his and tugged her against him. When her body melted against his, he smiled and planted a gentle kiss on her fingers.

"But I found I like it, *really* like it, when you're mouthy. Especially when you—"

Eve reached up and gently silenced him with a kiss, and with their lips still touching she breathed, "I'm scared."

"Yeah, me too—"

"No." Her voice hitched as she pressed her forehead against his cheek. "I'm really…*really* scared."

Chase felt an enormous relief flood though him. His fiery, fierce Eve was afraid. But that was okay. He was too. Afraid that he wouldn't be enough.

"I need you, Eve, more than I've needed anyone. And I think… I think you need me too."

She tensed for a fraction of a second, then her arms slid around him and she clung.

"It's too soon," she murmured against his throat, and a shudder of pure need flowed through him.

He shook his head. "No, it's not. I waited a long time for you, Dr. Carmichael, and I'm not letting you go."

"It's impossible," she said fretfully. "Two people don't fall in love in a fortnight. That's...r-ridiculous."

His heart stopped, then began a slow slog through his body. Had he heard her correctly? "*Two* people, Eve?"

She froze for a couple of heartbeats and then she tried to move away, but he tightened his arms around her.

"No. *No*. I...I just meant that it isn't possible for anyone to fall in love so fast."

"You have no idea," he admitted softly, and when she made a distressed sound in her throat he chuckled, pressing a kiss against her forehead. "Yep," he murmured. "Right about the time you opened your eyes and called me the pilot from hell."

Her head shot up and she gaped at him. "But...but..." she spluttered. "That's crazy. You didn't even *like* me."

"Maybe not." He chuckled. "But I *wanted* you like crazy. I still do. But you have to say it first."

She stilled. He saw her throat convulse before she turned her gaze to the huge rising moon. It dazzled him, that silvery glow that turned her amber eyes luminous.

"It must be the moon," she murmured.

He gaped at her. "The moon? What does the moon have to do with anything?"

"Seems I'm crazy too," she murmured, lifting her face. She brushed her lips against his. "Crazy about a sexy, grumpy pilot who crashed his seaplane in paradise."

He spluttered out a laugh. "Grumpy? You're calling me grumpy?"

"You forgot sexy," she murmured, sucking his lip into her mouth and then giving it a little nip.

He murmured something and caught her mouth in a punishing kiss. When they were both breathless, he broke it off and leaned his forehead against her.

"I'm crazy about you, Eve, and when you leave here I'm coming with you."

"You can't. This is your home." She gasped, taking his face between her palms. "I couldn't expect—"

"I can work—live—anywhere," he interrupted gently. "I just can't live without *you*."

"Why me?"

"You're it for me, Eve, and where you go, I go."

"What…what are you saying, Chase?"

Chase's smile turned tender. "I'm saying you're my everything. I'm saying I want to be your everything too."

For an instant she squeezed her eyes closed, and when she opened them again they sparkled with unshed tears. "You are. Don't you know that you are? That's why I was terrified," she admitted. "Terrified it was all just me."

"It's not. Never again. And if you still want to go to Washington—well, I'll just have to tag along."

"It doesn't have to be DC," she assured him gently. "It isn't the only city with great hospitals."

"No," he said. "It's not. In fact there's a great clinic right here on the island that needs another doctor. Or you could apply in Seattle, it's where I'm from and where my parents live, but I can run my business from anywhere in the world. All I need is a computer and internet access."

"You need a computer and internet access to fly a seaplane?"

Chase snorted. "Nope. I run an online brokerage firm, which is great because wherever you go I go." He cupped her face. "Anyone would be crazy not to snap you up in an instant, Eve. You know that, don't you?"

"I love you, Chase. It doesn't matter where I go. I just… I really want to be *your* everything too."

"Then let's go."

Her eyes widened. "What? Now?"

Chase laughed and turned her toward the house, suddenly lighter and happier than he could remember being. He tucked her against his side and pressed a kiss to her forehead, reveling in the way she pressed close.

"Later. I'll show you later how crazy I am about you. But right now Jude is opening a bottle of champagne. Right now I have to go ask your dad's permission."

"Wha-at?" she spluttered on a laugh, and he paused to snatch the lighthearted sound with his mouth.

"Yeah. It's what the guy does," he murmured when they were both breathing hard. "He asks the girl's dad's permission. I want to do this right, Eve, because…this feels right. *We* feel right."

"Yes," Eve said, smiling up at him and looking so beautiful she took his breath away. She took his hand, lacing their fingers together. "Yes, we do."

* * * * *